THE WESTERLEA HOUSE MYSTERY

ADAM CROFT

BOOKS IN THIS SERIES

Books in the Kempston Hardwick series so far:
1. Exit Stage Left
2. The Westerlea House Mystery

To find out more about this series and others, please head to adamcroft.net/list.

1

The bowl of sweets clinked and rattled as the long, slender digits plunged in to retrieve a handful of sugar-laced goodness.

'Oh, for Christ's sake!' the man exclaimed, throwing his treasure back into the bowl with a clink and a clatter. 'I specifically said no blue ones!'

The make-up artist peered enquiringly over his shoulder as their eyes met in the mirror.

'Sorry, Mr Whitehouse. It's not really my remit, but I'll go and find the person responsible.'

'No, no. Leave it,' the man replied, his eerie tones reminiscent of Vincent Price, or so she thought. 'Not much point now. I'll be on in five minutes anyway. Honestly, the whole thing has been a shambles. I clearly asked them for Belmore Hills spring water, and they gave me Shaffington Falls! I mean, why should I bother requesting a rider if you're only going to ignore it?'

'Mmmm, I know. Terrible,' the make-up artist responded, her attention focused purely on the dark powder that she was applying to his eyes. Each time she had met him, he had insisted on being made to look eerie, as he had phrased it. She was quite sure that his un-made-up face looked far eerier than anything she could ever muster with her GNVQs and GHDs.

'Three minute call, Mr Whitehouse. We'll be starting in just a mo,' the balding head said as it peered around the half-open door, its face far cheerier than it needed to be.

Oscar Whitehouse instinctively checked his watch. Although he couldn't stand being late for anything, he also had a particular dislike for over-exaggeration.

'Right. I think that's eerie enough, thank you, Charlotte. I'd best be heading through,' he said to the make-up artist.

'Right you are, Mr Whitehouse,' she replied. 'Knock 'em dead!'

He paused briefly. 'Oh, I'll be doing far more than that, don't you worry.'

. . .

He squinted under the bright lights as the black-shirted production staff led him through the darkened wings before asking him to wait at the final door. The speech from inside the studio was now more than audible.

'So please give a very warm welcome to my guest, Oscar Whitehouse!'

The green lighting effects and creaking door noise, courtesy of the sound department, would have had Oscar Whitehouse convulsing at the sheer galloping insolence were it not for the camera now trained on his face. Turning to feign laughter at what he knew he must accept as absolutely hilarious, he raised his hand in a casual wave to the audience, shook the host's hand and sat down on the sofa.

'Good afternoon, Oscar. Did you like the welcome?' the bright orange host asked, his teeth gleaming like two rows of ivory soldiers.

'Oh, yes, absolutely. Very good indeed,' he replied, the blood now seeping from his heavily-bitten tongue. 'Very original.'

'Now, Oscar, you're known all over the country and, indeed, all over the world for your paranormal investigations and insight into the supernatural. What was it that first had you interested in the supernatural realm?'

Never been asked that one before, he thought to himself, before replying, graciously. 'Well, I remember one particular experience back when I was a young boy,' he said, before pausing for dramatic effect. 'I was lying in bed one night – I must have only been six or seven years old – and I recall having the overriding urge to sit bolt upright. When I did, I saw my grandmother standing at the end of my bed, telling me everything was going to be all right. When I woke up the next morning, my father told me that my grandmother had died in the night, at the exact time I saw her in my bedroom.'

The on-cue oohs and aahs from the audience were perfectly timed as Oscar Whitehouse reeled out the story for the hundredth time. He was always amazed that the press hadn't yet discovered that his grandmother was actually alive and well in a nursing home in Bognor Regis. (If 'well' could be used to describe a woman who dribbled constantly and was convinced that Richard Madeley was the devil incarnate.) Seven television sets later, the family had wisely decided that she'd be far better off with a radio, following which, she had taken up the notion that the Shipping Forecast was actually a daily dose of Nazi propaganda.

The interview carried on in its inane manner, and Oscar Whitehouse continued to discuss his new book, Life After Death: A History of Supernatural Activity in the Afterlife, in a thinly-veiled manner only ever seen on daytime television.

'Now, you've been on our screens for a few years, and have taken part in hundreds, if not thousands of paranormal investigations,' the host continued, shifting to cross his legs the other way for the umpteenth time that minute. 'And your book focuses almost solely on your belief that our spirits live on after death. Do you expect that this book will convince the nay-sayers that the paranormal world is real?'

Oscar Whitehouse chuckled as he rubbed at his fingernail. 'No, I expect there will always be cynics. However, I know that the world will soon have proof of life after death. That much is true. Evil will always live on.'

The oohs and aahs from the audience were well cued by the school-leaver in the black t-shirt, who flailed his arms at the front when wishing to elucidate any sort of audience reaction. A nervous chuckle from the host ensured that the interview moved on rather swiftly, and he turned to address camera five.

'Oscar Whitehouse, for the moment, thank you. Now,' the host began his sentence in his well-accustomed way. 'We're on the lookout for haunted houses all over the country for a new feature on this programme. Do you live in, or know of, a haunted house anywhere in Britain? Perhaps your house – or your friend's house – has its very own spooky spectre. If so, give us a call and we'll get you on for a chat later in the show.'

The host stood from his interview chair and made his way over to the maniacally-grinning potters whose whirring machinery graced the other side of the stage, ready and waiting for the next ten soul-destroying minutes of television.

Ellis Flint used to quite like Greensleeves. But, having been kept on hold for an interminable amount of time listening to the piece, he had seriously considered forgetting all about his reason for calling and instead subjecting the other party to an historical diatribe on how Henry VIII had tried (and, with hindsight, hilariously failed) to claim that he had written it. When the phone was finally answered, he decided that plan of action would be a little too heavy for a Friday afternoon, and instead reverted to his initial script.

'Oh, yes, hello there. I'm just calling about the piece you're doing on haunted houses. It's about a friend of mine, actually, who lives in a really spooky old house at Tollinghill. Used to be a rectory. The place gives me the creeps.'

The over-excitement of the production assistant on the other end of the phone seemed to indicate that take-up for this particular segment of the show had been disappointing at best. As a result, Ellis Flint was very quickly assured that he would be put through to the host in the next few moments.

Ellis smiled and sat back down to enjoy the rest of the programme.

2

The soothing and melancholic sounds of Chopin's Valse Op. 34 No. 2 in A Minor permeated the ears of Kempston Hardwick and danced around his head as he lay back in his armchair and exhaled the last of his Monte Cristo cigar.

He enjoyed time on his own. There were some who had a certain appeal, but on the whole he wasn't especially keen on people. The clock in the hallway of the Old Rectory chimed the hour as the lilting cello sounded the minor key, which always evoked such deep relaxation and reflection in Hardwick.

Hardwick sat bolt upright in his chair and glanced around the room as he tried to re-familiarise himself with his surroundings. The searing light blazed through the curtains as if they didn't exist, and the muted chattering from outside became apparent. He switched off his gramophone and walked towards the window.

'Well, it's handy that we happened to be very near to Tollinghill, as it means we could come out and show the viewers the haunted location of the Old Rectory live on the programme!'

The young lady reporter spoke excitedly into her microphone as she shoved the earpiece further into her outer canal and gestured at the Old Rectory behind her.

'Now, this particular location was reported to us just a few minutes ago by local man, Ellis Flint, who stated in no uncertain terms that the Old Rectory is very haunted indeed.'

As she spoke, the young cameraman's face turned white and he pointed over her shoulder at the Old Rectory's downstairs living-room window. She turned to see the slender Victorian figure appear at the leaded glass.

The cameraman seized his opportunity and hopelessly zoomed in on the window, the wildly-changing focus sending small portions of the country into epileptic seizures. It was when he turned to tell the young lady reporter that he'd lost sight of the ghost, that he saw her sprinting off into the distance.

Assuming that his fifteen minutes of fame were over at the end of the original telephone call, Ellis Flint ambled into the kitchen to make himself a cup of tea. He opened the Post-It-note-laden cupboard door and took out his mug before pouring the contents of the freshly-boiled kettle into it. The cupboard door closed and 'Re-plant geraniums' fell into the brewing cup followed by 'Tidy workbench area' and 'Get haircut', which fell onto the Formica sideboard.

He scrambled to collect the falling Post-It notes as he answered the ringing phone.

'Ellis, it's Hardwick here.'

'Get a bloody haircut?' Ellis exclaimed as he examined the Post-It note in more detail.

'I beg your pardon?'

'Sorry, Kempston. Just trying to wade my way through a sea of Post-It notes Mrs F has decided to leave for me.'

'I see. Does she often do that?'

'Oh yes.'

'Right. Well. I realise this may sound a tad bizarre,

Ellis, but do you have any idea why there might be a television crew stood on my front lawn?'

'Uh... no,' Ellis replied, suddenly realising exactly why that might be. 'Why are you asking me?'

'Just an inkling, Ellis. Just an inkling...

The long summer afternoon finally gave way to the evening. The sun glowed on the edge of the Greensand Ridge to signal the beginning of the end of another successful day. Oscar Whitehouse's key rattled in the lock of the front door at Westerlea House before the tell-tale sound of the mortice bolt ratcheting back told Oscar that he was home and dry. As home and dry as he was likely to be with his wife, Eliza, standing a few steps from the bottom of the stairs with a glare of anger and suspicion on her face.

The long ivory dressing gown cascaded off her curved hips and bosom, her long auburn hair nestled on top of her shoulders.

'Dare I ask?' she indeed asked, gliding down the last

few steps and arriving to meet her husband at the bottom.

'Ask what?' Oscar replied innocently as he took off his black suit jacket and hung it on the peg on the back of the door before bending down to untie his shoelaces.

'Where you've been, Oscar. Your interview was in London and it finished at five. It's a half-hour journey and it's now six-thirty. Where the hell have you been since then?'

'Just out and about. I had a meeting with Sandy afterwards.'

'Oh yes, of course. I thought that might have been the case,' his wife replied, folding her arms and exhaling heavily.

'Jesus Christ, Eliza, she's my PR girl! We do need to have occasional meetings, you know.' Oscar shoved his hands into his pockets and headed for the solace of the kitchen.

'Just like you needed to have "occasional meetings" with Emma? And Tracy? And Candy?' she asked, her voice tautening with each mention of her husband's previous flings as she watched him pop a couple of ibuprofen out of the blister pack.

'Oh, for crying out loud, love. I've told you a number of times. There is nothing going on with Sandy! She's the one who gets me these TV gigs and keeps my career going. What's so wrong with that? You'd soon have more to complain about if I had no work and you couldn't go out three times a week to buy new shoes and handbags!'

Eliza's body language changed dramatically as she walked the last two steps to face her husband.

'No, Oscar. That woman does not keep your career going. I keep your career going. Now you had very well better remember that, because she might not always be here, and neither will you. I, on the other hand, will.'

Oscar, clearly in no mood for Eliza's histrionics, moved her firmly aside, saying: 'Now, if you'll excuse me, I'm going to bed. I feel bloody awful and my throat's red raw,' and laboured his way up the stairs.

'There really has been some mistake,' Hardwick finally managed to say as the crucifixes were lowered and the television reporters appeared from behind the rhododendrons. 'This house isn't haunted and I'm not a ghost.'

'You look like one,' said a timid voice from inside the conifer.

'Well I'm not. My name is Kempston Hardwick, I live in the Old Rectory and I have done for a number of years. There are absolutely no ghosts here whatsoever.' Hardwick walked the few extra feet across the gravel to the rather expensive-looking camera that stood on its tripod on his lawn, knowing that its operator would dash out of hiding to protect it within nanoseconds. He was right.

'Please don't touch the camera, sir!' a young man

with long hair and three-day growth on his chin said. 'It's a very expensive piece of equipment.'

'Oh, well there's nothing to worry about, surely. Ghosts can't touch things.'

The camera operator looked at Hardwick for a moment, unsure as to where the joke was, before letting out a cover-all half-laugh and relaxing slightly.

'Look, could we at least say it's haunted? It'll make really good TV!'

'No. Absolutely not. Besides, it seems you already have said it's haunted, without even bothering to speak to me. So if you'd be so kind, I'd like it if you could all go away as quickly as possible. I don't want any more of my time wasted on fatuous ghost stories.'

Those who had begun to pack up their equipment stopped doing so and looked at the camera operator as their designated spokesperson.

'Yeeess?' Hardwick enquired, somehow sensing that perhaps there was something he still hadn't been told.

'Well, we can't exactly just stop everything, sir.'

'How do you mean?'

'It's... it's kind of... it's all over Twitter.'

'What is?' Hardwick asked, not within a light year of being a Twitter user, but at least having some understanding of what it was.

'This, about your house,' the camera operator replied, flicking the zip on his hold-all. 'It's trending.'

Hardwick stood silently for a moment. 'So let's just make sure we're on the same page, here. You mean to say that the world and his mother now think my house is one of the most haunted locations in Britain?'

The camera operator's eyes darted about nervously. 'That's about the gist of it, yes.'

The doorbell rang cheerily through the house as Eliza Whitehouse clip-clopped her way across the parquet flooring in her stiletto heels to answer the door. The exuberant round face of Reverend Michael Winton greeted her as she stepped aside to let him through.

Michael Winton had been the vicar at the Church of St. Winifred the Colossal for almost thirty years and was known throughout the community as a man of the highest moral integrity. Throughout the Church's times of trouble and turmoil, the vicar remained as its revered representative in Tollinghill. No-one knew how old he really was; the inherent aura of authority around men of the cloth can often make it difficult to judge.

'Hello, Eliza,' the vicar said jovially as he greeted her in the European manner, with a kiss on each cheek and a hand on each shoulder. 'So lovely to see you. Am I the first one?'

'As always, vicar,' Eliza joked. Reverend Michael's penchant for timekeeping was well-known locally. Should a party be stated as starting 'from 8pm', the host knew full well that the vicar's ringing of the doorbell would coincide perfectly with the eighth bell toll at the Church of St. Winifred the Colossal.

'Oscar's upstairs at the moment. He's not feeling too well, unfortunately,' she added.

'Oh dear,' the vicar replied. 'There's a lot of it about at the moment, it seems. Only last week old Mrs Enderby was taken ill during one of my sermons. Right over my cassock.'

'How terrible. Harry not with you?' Mrs White-house asked hopefully.

'Just a few moments behind. He won't be long,' the vicar replied.

Harry Greenlaw, Tollinghill's young resident verger was a queer figure to many in the village, appearing, as he did, in a range of Gothic outfits when-ever ecclesiastical clothing did not apply. With his hair dyed jet black and his eyes adorned with eye-liner, he could be more easily mistaken for a follower of the dark forces, rather than of God Almighty. Regardless, he was clear in his dedication to the church and seemed not to allow fashion to dictate his metaphysical beliefs.

The rubbery squeak of the training shoes on the parquet flooring reminded Eliza Whitehouse of her only other party-goer thus far.

'You remember my son Andrew, don't you, vicar?'

'Why yes, of course!' he exclaimed rather too enthu-siastically, leaving Eliza and her son wondering whether or not this was entirely true. 'So lovely of you to have arranged such a fantastic party for your parents. You were knee-high to a grasshopper when I last saw you! You must have been... oooh, how old were you?'

'Seventeen,' Andrew replied.

'My, don't they grow up fast nowadays?' the vicar remarked to no-one in particular. 'So how is Oxford treating you?' he asked, belying his previous lapse of memory.

'Very well, thanks,' Andrew replied.

'What are you reading?' asked the vicar.

'PPE,' he replied, adding, 'Philosophy, Politics and Economics,' in response to the vicar's blank gaze.

'Philosophy, blimey. I presume you'll be familiar with St. Augustine and Thomas Aquinas, then?' the reverend asked, as Eliza shoved a glass of Prosecco into his hand.

'A passing familiarity, yes. I don't tend to go in much for religious philosophy, I'm afraid.'

The vicar seemed, at first, rather taken aback before replying, 'Yes, well. Catholics, the pair of them, so I'm not surprised.'

Quite unsure as to what to say in response to this remark, Eliza Whitehouse instead opted to lead Rev. Michael into the kitchen. As she did so, the doorbell rang out for a second time; Andrew Whitehouse this time opened the door to reveal Harry Greenlaw, resplendent in a shaped black button-up shirt and black combat-style trousers.

'Andrew! Lovely to see you. How's university?' the verger asked in a manner quite at odds with his appearance. Andrew doubted that Harry Greenlaw used the same approach to manners and articulation when he was with his underworld peers.

'Fine, thanks. How's... the church?'

'Still standing,' Harry replied, laughing at his own joke. 'We've a Redemption Day fête next weekend. You should come along.'

'Well, I –'

Harry added: 'Although, I should imagine you'll be back at university by then, won't you?'

'Oh, yes. Absolutely. Well back.' Andrew replied,

ushering Harry Greenlaw into the kitchen to join the rest of the small, but lively, party.

By half-past-eight, the festivities appeared to be in full swing. The Whitehouse's immediate neighbours were in attendance: Dolores Mickelwhite lived to their immediate left, almost directly opposite the church, with Major Arnold Fulcrupp shoring up the defences to the right-hand side.

Dolores Mickelwhite was what some might call a typical 'village character' (in a village such as Tollinghill, however, the concept of character was somewhat distorted by the sheer concentration of peculiarity). She appeared to be un-ageable, her short, stringy, black hair clumped to her head like the claw of a JCB, not quite meeting the substantial rim of her large glasses. A new-age-style smock hung around her shoulders, seemingly ignorant of the blissful summer heat.

'And there are even some here in Tollinghill,' she added, in an attempt to revive the floundering conversation which had – unsurprisingly, considering her attendance – turned to the supernatural. 'In fact, I was watching that television programme earlier this afternoon and they had a reporter over at the Old Rectory. You must have seen it. Oscar was on it.'

Meeting a range of still-uninterested shaking heads, Dolores Mickelwhite continued, 'Oh yes, it was on the TV and everything! They reckon the place is haunted.'

'Well, it is hundreds of years old,' Rev. Michael retorted. 'And we all know what happened there all those years ago.'

'Exactly! I tell you, I could swear blind there was a figure in the downstairs window.'

'Probably just a stunt for the television, Dolores. I wouldn't worry yourself.'

'Oh, I don't know, vicar. I have a feeling... a feeling that something rather odd is abreast in Tollinghill.' Dolores Mickelwhite put her hands together and murmured a few words under her breath as the other partygoers looked awkwardly at each other.

Major Fulcrupp decided that he had found the perfect time to join the conversation.

'What bloody tosh.'

'I beg your pardon!' Dolores Mickelwhite cried, incredulous at the Major's insult.

'I mean, ghosts and ghoulies and all that nonsense. You really must stop it, woman. Never going to find yourself a husband if you go around spouting that sort of diarrhoea,' the Major said, flailing his arms about as if sowing the spring seed.

'And what makes you think I want a husband

exactly, Major? You're doing a damned fine job of putting me off men for life!'

'You say that as if you were ever attracted to them in the first place,' the Major sneered, turning away to take a sip of his red wine.

'What is that supposed to mean? Are you trying to insinuate something, Major Fulcrupp?'

The tense atmosphere was sensed by all who stood in the kitchen as Dolores took a step towards the Major.

'Exactly what I said,' he replied, refusing to make eye contact with her.

Dolores Mickelwhite said nothing, and instead simply shook her head and left the room.

'Bloody dyke lunatic.'

'There's no need for that, Major,' Rev. Michael said, noticing the increased pinkness in Major Fulcrupp's cheeks. The Major would not have looked half as ridiculous, were it not for his thinning crop of fiery orange hair and accompanying glow-in-the-dark moustache.

'Some people need to be told, vicar. Never had any of that sort of nonsense out in the Falklands. Wouldn't have lasted five minutes.' Turning to Eliza Whitehouse, he swiftly changed the topic of conversation. 'Still no Oscar?'

'No, he's really not feeling too good at all, I'm afraid.'

'Oh, nonsense. He really must at least come down

THE WESTERLEA HOUSE MYSTERY   25

and say hello. I mean, it is his party after all,' the Major replied.

'Well, I'm sure we can have another party when he's feeling better,' said the dutiful wife.

'I'll hear none of it. Wouldn't have had hide nor hair of it in the Army. Come on, now,' he said, heading for the kitchen door. 'I'll go up there myself and see that he's down here and ship-shape in no time.'

Eliza Whitehouse grabbed the Major's arm, immediately regretting doing so as soon as she saw the look on his face.

'Mrs Whitehouse, I do not appreciate being manhandled...' by a woman, Eliza finished in her own mind.

'I'm sorry, Major. It's just that he might be having a bath or sleeping outside of the covers. He's been having awful swings of temperature.'

'Sounds like sissy fever to me.'

'Yes, well. I'll tell you what. I'll go up and see how he is, and maybe he'll pop down for a bit. It'll have to be very brief, though.'

'Suits me, my dear. I was hoping to catch Newsnight, anyway.'

6

It was a full fifteen minutes later that the pale and ashen-faced Oscar Whitehouse half descended the stairs wrapped in his towelling dressing gown and sat on the step. The lights had been dimmed in order to ease his searing headache.

'I think he should get some medical attention, Eliza,' Harry Greenlaw said upon seeing him. 'He really doesn't look good, and the thing with the light is worrying me. My cousin had that – turned out to be meningitis.'

'The doctor came by earlier, actually. We did wonder about meningitis but he said there were no other symptoms. He reckons it's just a virus or a fever,' Eliza replied.

'Sissy fever,' Major Fulcrupp reaffirmed from the back of the room.

'Was it Doctor Harrison?' Harry Greenlaw asked, referring to Tollinghill's long-standing physician.

'No, we couldn't get through to him. Had to call for a locum from Shafford,' Eliza affirmed.

'Ah, out of hours, was it?'

'Most times are with Doctor Harrison,' Eliza Whitehouse replied, much to the amusement of the gathered party-goers.

'Well I must say, old chap, you're looking mighty pale. Even in this low light. Best get yourself back up to bed, eh?'

The Major's sudden caring tone took the other party-goers a little by surprise, but Eliza acquiesced to the best interests of her husband and moved to help him slowly back up the stairs.

'That's OK, Eliza – I can take Oscar back up to bed for you,' Harry Greenlaw said.

'No, it's fine, thank you, Harry. There's really no need.'

'Eliza, I insist. You've been working far too hard this evening. Why don't you sit down and enjoy a nice glass of wine?'

Eliza Whitehouse thought for a moment. 'Well, OK. But be gentle with him. He's not quite himself.'

'Stop fussing, woman. I'll be fine,' said Oscar White-house in his hoarse voice.

'Blimey, you don't sound good at all, Oscar. Let's get you back up to bed,' said the verger.

Eliza was quick to remonstrate. 'Don't talk, Oscar. You need to save your voice.'

With Oscar Whitehouse safely escorted back upstairs by the verger, the party continued downstairs in his absence. Dolores Mickelwhite was, by all accounts, a little on the tipsy side and made a point of informing all of the assorted male party-goers that she was a single woman and, indeed, had not "had it" for some time.

It was half-past-nine when Dolores Mickelwhite rushed down the stairs and announced in a panicked voice that she could hear signs of a struggle from inside Oscar Whitehouse's bedroom.

'It sounds like he's being murdered!' Dolores said, her face ashen white. 'I tried the handle but the door was locked!'

'Are you sure it was locked, Dolores?' Eliza asked, agitation creeping into her voice. 'Oscar never locks the bedroom door.'

'Yes, definitely! I even looked through the keyhole to see what was going on, but the key was in the lock.'

Eliza, Harry Greenlaw and Rev. Michael all headed upstairs, leaving an oblivious and out-of-earshot Major Fulcrupp standing outside the patio doors smoking his cigar, and regaling Andrew Whitehouse (as he was the only party-goer who had not escaped the Major's clutches) with tales of the Falklands.

Eliza, Harry and the vicar snapped into action – Eliza frantically tugging at the door handle to no avail.

'Stand back,' Harry Greenlaw said, and gave himself a three-step run-up before ploughing his boot into the lock panel of the door – once, twice, thrice, until the lock finally gave way, the door swinging back and clattering against the wall. Harry and Eliza heard the key jangling to the floor as it fell from inside the lock.

'It was locked from the inside,' the vicar observed, before his eyes rose to meet the sight of Oscar Whitehouse lying face up on the bed with a look of horror and anguish on his face. Harry Greenlaw was the first to approach and test for a pulse.

'He's dead,' the verger announced, with tears in his eyes.

7

The ringing of the telephone always stirred a slight rage within Hardwick. The frustration of being disturbed during a train of thought, no matter whom by or for what reason, gave him cause to see the telephone as something of a social enemy.

'Hardwick,' he said flatly as he picked up the trilling receiver.

'Hello, Hardwick. It's DI Rob Warner here, from Tollinghill Police.'

DI Warner had the impressive habit of making even an innocent greeting sound like a threat. Not waiting for a response, he continued. 'We need to speak to you regarding a murder case.'

'Oh yes?' Hardwick enquired, not expecting much

based on his previous encounters with DI Warner. Having Hardwick arrested earlier in the year for interfering with police business during a murder case, which he had ultimately solved, had not exactly endeared DI Warner to him.

'Yes. It's pretty local to you, actually — Westerlea House.'

'I see. Tell me, why are you asking me? After all, it's you who's the qualified detective,' Hardwick said with more than a hint of satire in his voice, as he sat back in his chair and inspected his almost immaculate fingernails.

'Well, I should've thought you'd know that. The Superintendent was very impressed with the work you did on the Charlie Sparks case last year, so I thought it might be a good idea to get you involved.'

'Your Superintendent? Well, you are modest, DI Warner.'

There was an audible sigh on the other end of the line. 'Do I really need to spell it out for you, Hardwick? You solved that case practically single-handed. You know that, and... and I know that,' Warner said, after a slight pause.

'Oh? Well that's news to me, Inspector. You see, I distinctly recall the newspapers having the impression that all the credit for that case was due to you.'

The front-page of the Tollinghill Echo was an image that Hardwick had no trouble in recollecting.

CHARLIE SPARKS MURDER CASE: SUSPECT ARRESTED AND CONVICTED INVESTIGATING OFFICER D.I. ROB WARNER TO RECEIVE GONG

As things had transpired, DI Warner hadn't received any sort of award or commendation; the newspaper later stated that the policeman had "modestly declined" such acclamation. Hardwick saw this as a sign that DI Warner did, after all, perhaps have some modicum of dignity about him.

'You know what the press are like, Hardwick,' Warner said. 'Anything for a bit of sensationalism. Anyway, things are a bit tricky in the force at the moment with regards to hiring outside help. All this funding malarky, y'know.'

Like many local police forces, the one that was charged with keeping the sleepy village of Tollinghill safe from ne'er-do-wells, was also under severe pressure to cut budgets in the midst of Britain's financial crisis, which came off the back of more than a decade of profligate public sector spending.

'I never asked for a penny of payment, Inspector, nor did I receive any.'

'No, but still. The whole practice is under scrutiny and I've got to be careful as to what gets back to my superiors. Bottom line is I want you involved.'

The whys and wherefores of murder and serious crime had always fascinated Hardwick. Ever since he was a young child he had sat open-mouthed as his father regaled him with tales from Dame Agatha Christie and Sir Arthur Conan Doyle. Christie's books, in particular, held a special kind of appeal, often concentrating, as they did, on modes of transport and crimes committed in faraway lands. This appealed greatly to Hardwick's own love of travel and foreign climes; things he'd become well accustomed to in his formative years.

'I see. What can you tell me about the case?' Hardwick asked.

'Not much at the moment. Not over the phone, anyhow. It might interest you to know that the deceased is—or was—Oscar Whitehouse.'

Hardwick paused for a moment, unsure of what he was meant to say.

'It doesn't, no.'

'I'm sorry?' asked the Inspector.

'It doesn't interest me to know that. I presume I should have heard of him?'

'Well, yes,' DI Warner replied. 'He's one of the most famous... Actually, never mind. Just get over to Westerlea House as quickly as you can, will you?'

It always struck Hardwick as quite incredible that such great swathes of the British public seemed to order their lives around celebrities: those who did a normal job (and a fairly easy or loosely-defined one at that), with the only exception being that they did so under the watchful eye of the general public. It seemed to Hardwick that this was a horrible notion, rather like having fifty-million bosses.

'Right. And what is it that you need from me, exactly, DI Warner?' Hardwick asked, now fully aware that there was only one boss in this particular situation.

'I told you, Hardwick. I need you to come over,' DI Warner said, his patience running thin.

'On what basis, Inspector?' Hardwick asked. 'Would I be right in saying that you need my help?'

The line went silent for a few moments.

'Just get over here now, Hardwick.'

Hardwick could almost hear Detective Inspector Rob Warner's teeth grinding from a distance of some fifty feet as he approached Westerlea House. A light scattering of browning leaves lined the short gravel driveway, which led to the imperious Warner and his wet sidekick, DC Sam Kerrigan.

'Ah, DI Warner. How lovely to see you again,' Hardwick said as he opened his arms in mock salutation.

'Hardwick. Pleased you could make it.'

Hardwick offered a non-committal murmur as he briefly recalled the last time he had met Detective Inspector Rob Warner. The death of Charlie Sparks, the former Saturday-night comedian and television personality had almost stumped Hardwick, and the distrusting and overbearing eye of DI Warner had helped very little at the time. He had, however, managed to solve (with the help of Ellis Flint) that particular case for Warner, and seemed to have rather endeared himself to the detective. Now, he realised, Warner needed him and he was going to make sure he reminded him of that little fact at every opportunity he got.

'I'll be honest,' Warner added. 'The moment I saw that old Oscar Whitehouse had died in a locked room with no means of escape other than the door, which had been bolted from the inside... I couldn't hang around on it. I'd usually not bother, but, well... it seemed like it might be right up your street. No time to waste, and all that. I need a result on this, Hardwick. The Super's already on my back about blinkin' standards and protocols.'

Hardwick smiled as he thought himself lucky to be mostly free of the red tape, protocols and paperwork, which burdened the lives and working practices of the modern day police officer. His only concern was that the person responsible was caught and that their culpability could be proven.

'For some reason, the Super thinks that DI Warner was a bit... sloshed,' DC Sam Kerrigan added.

'Sloshed, DC Kerrigan?' Hardwick asked, his head cocked to one side.

'Yeah. Mentioned something about DI Warner and a piss-up in a brewery.'

'Yes, thank you, DC Kerrigan,' Detective Inspector Warner said, briskly, as he shepherded Hardwick towards the front door of Westerlea House, at which point Hardwick stopped in his tracks.

'Ah, no. I'm afraid I'm going to need to take a look on my own, Detective Inspector,' Hardwick said.

'I'm sorry, Hardwick. You know I can't allow that.'

'Ah, well, there seems to have been a mistake,' Hardwick said, turning to head back up the driveway. 'Do give me a call if you need me for anything else, Inspector.'

Warner sighed as he thrust his hands into the pockets of his suit trousers and called out in an exasperated voice. 'Hardwick. Wait.'

Hardwick stopped walking, his hands deep in the pockets of his overcoat and waited, eyebrows raised and eyes rolled upwards in anticipation.

'OK,' Warner said. 'The SOCO boys should have done their job by now. Not that they're likely to find anything — marks on his neck looks like the killer wore gloves. The witnesses are all to stay within that house, in sight of my officers, understood? You've got five minutes.'

'I'll be down in four,' Hardwick replied, as he passed DI Warner and headed back through the front door.

Hardwick whistled the opening bars of a Mozart opus to himself as he followed the young constable's directions towards the sweeping staircase of Westerlea House. He noted the enormous, regal — and slightly pretentious — oil paintings (Hardwick suspected reproductions) of various ancestors and previous incumbents of the residence.

The downstairs hallway of Westerlea House was a large, open-plan affair, with the long, sweeping staircase rising up the right-hand wall before turning left at a ninety-degree angle onto the U-shaped upstairs landing — also open. The landing covered three sides of the hall-way, the only exception being the front wall, which was a large, open and scaled both storeys of the house.

On the ground floor, as Hardwick had walked through the front door, he had noticed the dining room to his immediate right, with another door further along the right-hand wall. To his left was a sitting room, with a second door further along that wall. The kitchen and conservatory seemed to cover most of the back of the house.

Upstairs, Hardwick noted a number of doors – most of them guest bedrooms or storage space, the constable told him – one of which was wide open and led to a room at the back of the house, over the kitchen.

As they reached the open door to Oscar White-house's bedroom, Hardwick stopped for a moment in order to survey the scene. He had long been of the opinion that no detail was too small to consider.

'It was locked from the inside,' the voice said, as Reverend Michael Winton gave his apologies to the police officer who had been taking his statement and left the room to greet Hardwick. 'The key was on the floor. We heard it fall.'

Hardwick nodded, saying nothing.

The vicar was in casual dress. Casual, that is, for a clergyman. He wore his shirt and dog-collar (Hardwick presumed them compulsory), over which he had a green v-neck jumper. Although his hair was greying considerably, Hardwick supposed that he couldn't have been much over the age of forty.

'Looks as though he's been strangled,' the vicar added, offering a very British interruption to the dreaded two-second conversational silence.

'How so?' Hardwick enquired, making eye contact with the clergyman for the first time.

'Well, he's got two enormous great red hand-prints on his neck and his eyes are practically bulging from their sockets... I'm sorry, you should probably see for yourself. This isn't doing me any good at all.'

If a vicar could not deal with death, Hardwick thought, who could?

On entering the room, Hardwick could not help but be drawn to the seemingly possessed figure of Oscar Whitehouse, laid out on the bed to the left-hand side of the room, with his head cocked slightly toward the window opposite the door. His long, bony index finger appeared to be pointing towards it; an eerie indicator, which seemed to have gone unnoticed by the other parties.

'This window,' Hardwick asked, walking over to it. 'Does it open?'

'Uh, you'll have to ask his wife, Eliza, I'm afraid. I'm not altogether familiar with the house,' Rev. Michael Winton replied.

'And where is Mrs Whitehouse?' Hardwick asked as he jiggled the latch, which seemed to be stuck fast.

'She ran off downstairs when we saw the body,' the vicar explained. 'I can imagine it would be a terrible shock for her. I heard her being comforted by the Major, downstairs. Go down and check she's all right, will you, Harry? I think the police have a family liaison chap there, but best to see she's all right.'

The verger, Harry Greenlaw, acquiesced and daintily shuffled his shaking self across the landing and towards the staircase.

Hardwick ran his fingers around the frame of the window, as if seeking a draught. 'The window hasn't been open for quite some time. A matter of years, I'd say.'

'How do you know that?' the vicar asked. 'And why do you need to ask Eliza if you already know? Can't you see she's been through such a –'

Hardwick interrupted him. 'Because interpretation is a wonderful thing, vicar, but it doesn't equal fact. No, I can tell the window has been inaccessible for some time as the paint fills the gaps between the window and the frame. Rather careless and slipshod handiwork if you ask me, but rather useful for me in this instance. Had the window been opened since it had been painted, the paint would have broken and cracked slightly where it meets the frame. The window clearly hasn't been opened since the frame was painted. Tell me, vicar, was Oscar Whitehouse a smoker?'

'No, I can't say he was, why?'

'And Mrs Whitehouse?'

'No, she despised smoking. In fact, I'm pretty sure no-one in the house smokes at all. Especially not inside the house. It's always kept so clean. Why are you asking?'

'Because the paint on the window frame is quite yellowed. Of course, it happens to the best of paints over time, but a smoker in the room would accelerate the process quite considerably. Taking that out of the equation, I'd estimate it's been almost ten years since this window was last painted and therefore opened.'

The footsteps grew louder as the now-widowed Eliza Whitehouse, and Major Arnold Fulcrupp, came towards the bedroom. Having stopped short of the door, the Major put a reassuring hand on Eliza's back and cocked his head slightly towards her.

'I'm not going in there until they've moved him, Arnold!' the voice of Eliza Whitehouse cried. 'I can't... bear... to see him like that!' Sobs of desperation interspersed her speech as she fell into the embrace of Major Fulcrupp just out of sight of Hardwick and Rev.

Michael Winton. Hardwick moved towards the doorway.

'Mrs Whitehouse, I'm terribly sorry for your loss,' Hardwick said, getting the formalities out of the way rather quickly and abruptly. 'Tell me, do you know when the bedroom window was last opened?'

Eliza Whitehouse was slightly taken aback by Hardwick's direct route of questioning. 'Well, no. Not since we've lived here. We never could work out how to get the thing open. Oscar tried to... Oh! It's just too terrible!' she cried, as she fell into another fit of hysterical sobbing, this time on the shoulder of a rather awkward and uncomfortable Hardwick.

'Mrs Whitehouse, did you live here alone with your husband?' Hardwick said, as his hand hovered mere centimetres from Eliza Whitehouse's spine, unsure whether (and how) he should comfort her.

'Yes, most of the time. Our son, Andrew, is home from university, but that's only for a few weeks of the year. Otherwise we live here alone. Even more alone now... now...' she sobbed.

'Yes, well. What about extended family? Do any live close by?'

'I have two sisters, Maria and Louise. They live in Fettlesham, about three doors away from each other. Oscar was an only child.'

At this, Eliza Whitehouse burst into another uncontrollable flow of tears and left the room, accompanied by the young Harry Greenlaw, who had been waiting outside the room. The young police constable stood awkwardly just inside the doorway.

The vicar spoke. 'I'm sorry. I can imagine it must have been a terrible shock for her.'

'I see,' replied Hardwick – obliviously – a superabundance of thoughts flowing through his mind. 'And does anybody else visit the house regularly? A cleaner or gardener, perhaps.'

'Well, yes,' the Rev. Michael Winton said, his feet shuffling awkwardly as he spoke. 'There is the gardener. He only comes on Wednesdays, mind.'

'Five days ago,' Hardwick said, to no-one in particular.

'Yes. He'll be back the day after tomorrow if you need to speak to him. Christos Karagounis, his name is.'

'I'm afraid I'll need to speak to him sooner than that, vicar. I don't suppose it has passed your notice that this is now a murder investigation.'

'Well, yes, quite. I... um... I suppose his telephone number must be in Eliza's address book, somewhere,' the vicar replied, clearly uncomfortable at the thought of having to rifle through Eliza Whitehouse's possessions at such a delicate moment.

'There's no need,' the voice from the door said, now seemingly calm and placated. 'He lives in Shafford. On the King's Road.'

'I see. Thank you, Mrs Whitehouse, and thanks for your help, vicar. If you don't mind, I'd like to take a few moments to...' Hardwick trailed off as he gestured to the empty room. Rev. Michael Winton understood the implicit meaning and headed off downstairs, escorting Eliza Whitehouse.

As Hardwick stood in the doorway of the bedroom, he noted the solid brass key, which lay on the wooden floor a couple of feet from the threshold. Noting that it had already been dusted for fingerprints, he picked it up and placed it in the lock. Hardwick turned the key and the latch clicked into place, confirming it was in full working order. As he faced the inside of the room, Hardwick could see Oscar Whitehouse's grand four-poster bed, the head of which rested against the left-hand wall, a small bedside table placed either side.

The body of Oscar Whitehouse lay on the bed, his eyes half open and his jaw drooping in a state of final rest. His face was congested with blood, his neck marked with handprints and the indentation of a forearm across the front of his throat. Unplanned manual strangulation at its finest. The handprints were too irregular to suggest bare hands; gloves were far more likely. Hardwick supposed that considering the force required to hold a fully-grown man down in his bed and throttle him, the murderer was most likely a man. That is, of course, assuming that Oscar Whitehouse was in the peak of health just before his murder.

With the large window taking up the majority of the rear wall, Hardwick's attention turned to the right-hand wall, which included a walk-in wardrobe recess at the rear corner, next to which stood a stunning Georgian dresser. A brass candelabra adorned the centre of the piece, with a small brass bowl to the right of it and a lace doily to the left. On the near side of the right-hand wall, the door to the en-suite bathroom was ajar.

On the floor between the dresser and the en-suite door, lay a dark blue dressing gown. As Hardwick picked the dressing gown up, he noticed a small brass hook on the floor next to it. Hardwick picked up the hook and examined it, and then looked up. Indeed, just to the left of the en-suite door Hardwick noted a small sticky tab attached to the wall. The screw holes in the hook matched the indentations on the sticky tab perfectly. He smiled as he silently approved of the Whitehouses' approach in leaving walls unsullied by screws and nails. He pressed the hook back onto the sticky tab and hung the dressing gown back up on the wall before entering the en-suite bathroom.

The bathroom – being at the front of the room – sided onto a spare bedroom, backed onto the walk-in wardrobe, and fronted the landing. That being the case, Hardwick found no window in the en-suite, but was instead blinded by the intense halogen lighting that had been installed. The bathroom was otherwise fairly prosaic, consisting of a toilet, over-bath shower (the bath part of which had, presumably, Eliza Whitehouse's ivory dressing gown draped over it), sink and a small cabinet containing towels and other bathroom sundries.

After examining the bathroom, Hardwick made a quick search of the walk-in wardrobe and satisfied himself that there was no more to be seen.

DI Warner approached Hardwick as he descended the stairs.

'So what've you found, Hardwick?'

'A few things. I'll be sure to let you know once I've completed my investigation, Inspector.'

The short walk back to the Old Rectory was one which Hardwick barely noticed. He mulled over each of the little details in his mind as he meandered up Hill Lane. The trick, he knew, was knowing which of those little details could possibly be relevant. Each, in its own way, would have its significance, but knowing what to prioritise and what to mentally file as largely trivial was what he had to fathom.

He stepped carefully over the guy ropes and slalomed between the throngs of people on his front lawn before opening the solid oak front door and walking inside. Now in the hallway, he picked up the phone and called Ellis Flint.

'Ellis? It's Hardwick. How do you fancy a little intellectual stimulation?'

'Depends what you mean. I don't fancy another five-hour Countdown marathon, Kempston.'

'No, nothing of the sort. I've just been to see DI Warner. It seems there's been a murder in Tollinghill and he wants us—well, me—to help out.'

'Wow! Great! I mean... what's happened?'

'I can't tell you over the phone, Ellis. Nor can I divulge any details until you tell me why there are two hundred Chinese tourists presently camped out on my front lawn.'

'Chinese tourists? I don't know what you mean. Why would there be Chinese tourists in your garden?'

'I was hoping you could help me with that one, Ellis. It appears that it might be something to do with my house now being one of Britain's foremost tourist attractions for the world's ghost hunters.'

'Ghost hunters? Oh... yeah, that.'

'Yes. That,' Hardwick replied.

'Look, I didn't know they were going to put it on the telly, did I?' Ellis replied, shifting his weight awkwardly onto his other foot. 'They asked if there were any spooky locations, so I told them about the Old Rectory.'

'Ellis, the Old Rectory is not spooky. Nor did they ask you. They asked their audience. The sort of people who sit at home, with nothing better to do, phoning up fatuous daytime television shows to... Well, people like you, Ellis. Listen. Meet me at Westerlea House in twenty minutes. I'll be over as soon as I've written and handed out two hundred eviction notices. In Chinese.'

8

Ellis Flint arrived full of youthful exuberance. The chance to play detective again was just too good to turn down, and he had raced to Westerlea House as quickly as he possibly could. Then again, the chance to get away from Mrs Flint's cooking was a particular draw.

Hardwick greeted Flint and noted the spring in his step, hoping the assembled party-goers wouldn't take it in any spirit other than that in which it was meant. Although Hardwick often found Flint to be trying, he couldn't fault his knack for—amongst the daft and downright barmy comments—eventually managing to say or do something which would lead to a resolution. Thoughts of monkeys and typewriters came into Hardwick's mind.

'Mr Greenlaw, am I right in thinking you discovered the body?' Hardwick asked the verger.

'That's right, yes,' Harry Greenlaw replied, as he bowed his head. 'I was there with Michael and Eliza.'

'Would you mind if we spoke to you for a few moments in private?' Hardwick gestured towards the door and Harry Greenlaw assented, leading Hardwick and Flint into the dining room on the opposite side of the hallway.

'Now, in your own words please tell us exactly what happened tonight, Mr Greenlaw.'

'OK, well, I meant to arrive here at the same time as the vicar, Michael, but I got a little waylaid back at the vicarage. You see, I've got this new trouser press and it's got a little knob on the side that controls the amount of steam it produces. Well, obviously a lower setting is meant to produce less steam, but I think someone must have put the knob on incorrectly because when you turn —'

Hardwick interrupted, 'I see, so you pressed your trousers and followed the vicar to Westerlea House, yes?'

'That's correct, yes.'

'So tell me what happened just before Oscar White-house's body was found.'

'Well, I was sitting in the drawing room with Eliza,

Michael, and a few of the others. I distinctly remember admiring the crystal decanter on the drinks cabinet. Wonderful piece, it was. My father used to be a glass blower, you know? Taught me how to spot a decent piece of glassware and I've always been a fan of crystal. All homeware, in fact. I once had a turnip peeler, which –'

'Mr Greenlaw!' Hardwick implored. 'Please, will you cut to the chase and tell us what happened, briefly, without deviation, precisely from the moment that you realised Oscar Whitehouse was dead.'

'Well,' the verger thought for a few moments, clearly wanting to get this right. 'He wasn't breathing.'

'Oh, for crying out loud...'

'Mr Greenlaw,' Ellis Flint interrupted, placating Hardwick with a hand on his knee, which stunned the latter into silence. 'Were you downstairs when you realised that something was wrong?'

'Oh yes. We were in the drawing room and Dolores came running downstairs, shouting something about hearing a struggle in the master bedroom and not being able to open the door. Eliza, Michael and I went upstairs to see what all the fuss was about.'

Hardwick looked askance at Flint, amazed by Harry Greenlaw's sudden specificity of conversation.

'I see,' Flint continued. 'How long was Dolores

Mickelwhite absent from the party downstairs before she called down?'

'I can't be sure. She said she was going to use the toilet, but that was a good few minutes earlier.'

'And what did you find when you went upstairs?'

'Well, the door was locked. The key wasn't in the outside of the lock so we barged the door open.'

'And where was Oscar Whitehouse?'

'Sprawled on the bed, dead,' he replied, wringing his hands so hard that Hardwick could see the pink flesh yellowing.

'I see. And can you be completely sure that no-one other than Oscar Whitehouse was in the room? Did you check everywhere?'

'No, but the police did. And there was... someone in the room the whole time from finding him to them arriving,' the verger said, reluctantly.

'And who was that person, Mr Greenlaw?'

Harry Greenlaw paused for a few moments, clearly uncomfortable, before saying, 'Michael. The vicar.'

9

'Ah, Mrs Mickelwhite, isn't it?' Hardwick asked as he entered the living room to find a solemn but visibly shaking Dolores Mickelwhite. She was clearly no spring chicken, but seemed to be in that awkward forty-five-to-sixty-five age range, in which many women appear to be of completely indeterminate age. Her eyes practically bulged under the thick lenses of her glasses, and her dark but greying hair matted to her head.

'Ms, yes,' she replied. Hardwick was momentarily taken aback by the woman's desire to confuse rather than clarify, but continued unabashed.

'I hope you don't mind, but my colleague and I need to ask you a few questions,' Hardwick said, gesturing to Ellis as he sat down in the armchair next to the large, ornate fireplace. He took a moment to admire his surroundings: the sort of large country sitting room in which he'd feel very much at home.

'No, I don't mind at all,' the woman said, wiping the bottom of her eyes with her index fingers.

'The other partygoers tell me it was you who raised the alarm. Can you tell us a little more about that?'

'Well, yes, it was me. I was outside the bedroom door and I could hear a struggle inside. Oh, God, it was horrible! It sounded like a gurgling drain. Someone was grunting and breathing heavily, the bed was banging, and then all of a sudden it stopped. It's not a set of sounds I'm familiar with at all.'

'Ms Mickelwhite, did you say anything or make any sort of noise when you were outside the door?'

'I think I probably did. I couldn't believe what I'd just heard, so I would imagine that I made some sort of noise.'

'Ah. In which case, when you went downstairs to raise the alarm, the killer would have had — what — the best part of a minute to escape?'

'Escape where, though? There were other people downstairs — it was a party — besides, the bedroom door was locked from the inside when we got back up there!'

'Both the police and I searched that room high and low, Ms Mickelwhite. There was no-one else in it.'

'Impossible! I heard someone! I mean, a man can't strangle himself! Can he...?'

'Technically, yes, although that's not what happened here. The position and direction of the hand prints show that he was definitely strangled by someone else. Ms Mickelwhite, please enlighten me: what were you actually doing outside Oscar Whitehouse's bedroom door in the first place?'

Dolores Mickelwhite went silent for a few moments, having somehow neglected to consider that this question would be asked.

'I just went for a walk, really,' she said, smiling with over-enthusiastic confidence.

'Ms Mickelwhite, you live in Tollinghill. We're surrounded by rolling hills and lush woodland. When I quite fancy going for a walk, I tend to take a stroll over the hills, or through one of our many well-kept parks. I don't tend to do circuits of people's upstairs landings.'

Dolores Mickelwhite's head dropped slightly, realising that her excuse had completely and utterly failed her.

'It was what he said on that television programme,' she said reluctantly. 'About having proof of life after death. I've always been interested in the paranormal and wanted to know what he meant. I was... Well, I guess I was being nosy.'

'You were snooping, Ms Mickelwhite,' Hardwick affirmed.

'Well, yes. I suppose I was. But is that such a crime? It certainly doesn't make me a murderer!'

'It does, though, put you at the scene of the crime.'

'Well, yes, but... but why would I kill Oscar White-house, then come downstairs and tell everybody?' she asked, clearly accepting the understandable suspicion, but keen to clear her name.

Hardwick was silent for a few moments.

'Well, thank you for your time, Ms Mickelwhite. We'll be in touch should we need to speak to you further.'

10

Major Fulcrupp stood to attention as Hardwick and Flint entered the dining room to speak with him. He was dressed all in tweed, much the former-military man now enjoying a relaxing country retirement.

'Terrible business, this,' the Major said as he shook hands firmly with Hardwick and Flint. A little too firmly, Ellis thought, as he felt the bones crunch under Major Fulcrupp's iron grip. 'Would never have happened in the Army.'

'People never die in the Army, Major?' Hardwick enquired with a sense of sarcasm.

'Well, no, of course they do. What I mean is that in the Army we all looked out for each other. A loose cannon like that wouldn't have lasted five minutes in the barracks. If you've never been in the Army you wouldn't understand, lad. It's a way of life.'

'Agreed,' Ellis Flint added, smiling audaciously at Hardwick.

'Oh, you were in the Army?' the Major asked.

'Yes, for a short time. A couple of years back.'

'Ah, I see. Baghdad? Kabul?'

'Pirbright,' Ellis answered.

'Ah,' the Major said, with a slight air of condescension. 'So you didn't see any action?'

'Not all that much. I was in the Royal Logistics Corps. We weren't called into action while I was there.'

'He spent two weeks as a cook, Major, now can we get down to business?' Hardwick interjected, leaving Ellis Flint feeling mightily embarrassed. 'Where were you exactly when Dolores Mickelwhite sounded the alarm?'

'In the back garden, smoking, it seems. We didn't actually know anything was going on at the time as the conservatory door was closed, so we didn't hear the commotion.'

'We?' Ellis Flint asked.

'Yes, I was outside with Andrew, Oscar and Eliza's son. He was asking about my old Army days.'

Hardwick and Flint somehow knew that Andrew

Whitehouse hadn't technically asked about anything, but that the Major had gone off on yet another trip down memory lane.

'I see,' Hardwick said. 'So when did you first know that something had happened?'

'Well, I finished smoking my cigar and came back indoors. We realised everyone had disappeared, except Dolores who was in the kitchen. She was in a right old state, arms everywhere. I got the gist of what was going on and told her to stay downstairs with Andrew. By the time I got upstairs it had pretty much all finished. That's when we called the police.'

'So the door was already unlocked when you got up there?' Hardwick asked.

'Well, it was open. They'd kicked it open, by all accounts. Dolores said that she'd looked through the keyhole before they did, and that she could clearly see the key still on the inside of the lock.'

Hardwick paused for a few moments and rested his chin on his hand as Ellis Flint scribbled furiously into his red leather-bound notebook. 'And did you see anything suspicious while you were outside at all? Any sort of movement? Anyone else in the garden?'

'Nothing at all,' the Major said. 'It was still fairly light, so we would've seen if someone had come past us.

You get a pretty good view of the garden from that decking area, so I can be quite sure no-one else was out there.'

'In which case, Major, the murderer must have still been in the house.'

11

Major Fulcrupp backed up Harry Greenlaw's story to the last word, so Hardwick and Flint turned their energies to interviewing Eliza Whitehouse, Oscar's wife.

Eliza sat on a kitchen chair, sipping from a mug of hot cocoa as Hardwick and Flint pulled out two more chairs — Ellis scraped his across the tiled floor with the sound of a dying elephant — before sitting down. Andrew Whitehouse had kindly made Hardwick and Flint a cup of tea each, checked his mother was placated and then left the trio to their conversation.

'Mrs Whitehouse, can you tell me a little bit about what happened earlier tonight?' Hardwick asked.

'Oscar had been feeling unwell all day, he said, so he went to bed shortly after he came in. I went up to check on him around nine-fifteen and he seemed all right. Very drowsy and not all that well, but I saw no reason to worry too much.'

'And for how long were you out of the drawing room altogether?'

'Not long, I don't suppose. I came straight up, went in to the bedroom, saw he was resting and came back downstairs.'

'And were you absent from the party at any other time?'

'No, not at all. I was downstairs through the whole evening.'

'Oooh,' Ellis Flint said.

'Yes? What is it?' Hardwick replied.

'Do you have any sugar?' Ellis asked Eliza.

'Erm...Yes, in the little terracotta bowl, there.'

Ellis stood up, reawakening the dying elephant and heaped four large tablespoons of sugar into his tea.

'Mrs Whitehouse, did anyone else go upstairs at all?' Hardwick asked.

'Not that I'm aware of, no. Well, except for one person.'

'Go on,' Hardwick implored.

'His PR girl—Sandy Baker—popped over to see how he was. She wasn't here for long at all, though, so I very much doubt that she was involved.'

'At what time was this? No-one else seems to have mentioned it.'

'She knocked while I was walking through the hall, so I let her in. Something about signing some contracts or something. As for the time, I didn't look at the clock. It was after Oscar came downstairs and before he –'

'Yes, I see.' Hardwick thought for a moment. 'And did anyone else see Oscar Whitehouse after Ms Baker visited him?'

'I'm not sure. I don't think so — apart from me — but I wasn't exactly watching the staircase the whole evening.'

Hardwick thanked Eliza Whitehouse for her time, told her he'd be in touch and ushered Flint out of the house. Then he turned on his heels and called out to Eliza.

'Oh, Mrs Whitehouse? Who was the doctor who came to visit your husband?'

'I'm not sure. Our usual doctor wasn't available, so they had to call for a locum. Dr Daniels sticks in my mind, but don't hold me to that.'

* * *

'So we can cross another name off the list, then,' Flint

said as he and Hardwick leant against a low wall next to Westerlea House.

'Hmmm?' Hardwick murmured, lost deep in thought.

'Well, if Oscar Whitehouse was seen alive after Sandy Baker's visit then she couldn't possibly have killed him.'

'And why-ever not?' Hardwick asked, rummaging in his jacket pockets for the cigars he knew he hadn't brought.

'Because he was still alive! And before you start on some theory that she must have done something to initiate his death, or that she slipped him some sort of poison, that's nonsense – he was strangled.'

'Oh, Ellis, really,' Hardwick said, shaking his head. 'Why must you always take everything at face value? You really must begin to look at the detail. Yes, Eliza Whitehouse knew that Sandy Baker had visited her husband, because she knocked on the door and announced herself. The difference between you and me is that you take it as implicit proof that Sandy could not have killed Oscar Whitehouse. To me, it says quite the opposite. Friday night was a warm night, and there were guests occasionally smoking at the back of the house. I very much doubt they would have bothered to keep the patio doors closed for the entire night, when it was still so warm outside. Perhaps when they were smoking in order to keep the smoke outside, but surely not once everyone was indoors. No, it wouldn't have been at all difficult for Sandy Baker to wait until the coast was clear and slip inside unnoticed. From thereon-in, it's remarkably easy for her to go upstairs and kill Oscar Whitehouse. And what's more, she appears to have the perfect cover by having already visited earlier that night. Who would ever assume she would come back, this time silently?'

'It's not a bad theory, Kempston, but the point still remains that whoever killed Oscar Whitehouse had to somehow get out of a room, which was locked from the inside, with that door as the only means of escape.'

'Yes, that would appear to present a slight problem, but I wouldn't worry too much about it just now,' Hardwick replied, pushing himself away from the wall and starting to walk back down Hill Lane.

'But why?' Ellis asked, following a few paces behind. 'Surely it's crucial to the case!'

'Not especially. Let's not worry ourselves about the means of murder and escape. The means can't kill again, Ellis. But the murderer can.'

12

The next morning, the heavy oak door of the vicarage opened with a slight creak to reveal the looming figure of Reverend Michael Winton, who greeted Hardwick and Flint with a smile and invited them to come inside. The vicar had that strange look that only vicars could have: the one which is both melancholic and reassuring at the same time. A trustworthy face, as Ellis's mother would have said.

As Hardwick and the vicar moved into the kitchen, Ellis Flint skulked slowly behind, picking up a few porcelain figures and closely inspecting the vicar's grandfather clock. 'Detail...' he murmured to himself as he noted the size and shape of the figures, as well as the manufacturer's details on the clock.

'What detail, Ellis?' came the voice of Hardwick, less than six inches from his ear.

Struggling with all his might to keep the porcelain cow airborne, Ellis quickly regained his composure. 'Oh, nothing. Just talking to myself.'

'I see. Well this is no time for porcelaneous bovine juggling, Ellis. Just a shame it's not a pig.'

'Sorry?'

'A porcelain pig, Ellis. Far more fitting than a cow. The word "porcelain" comes from the Italian porcellana and Latin porcellus, which is the diminutive of porcus – a pig. Technically, "porcelain" means "pig-like".'

'But it's a cow,' Ellis replied.

'Yes, yes. Come on, Ellis. The kitchen!'

The vicar turned to smile at Hardwick and Flint as they entered the kitchen, and poured the boiling water onto the tea leaves, revealing the musky scent of Darjeeling.

'Cup of tea?' the vicar asked, having already poured three cups.

It looks like it, doesn't it? Hardwick wanted to answer, but settled for 'Yes please, Father.'

'Please, call me vicar. Even better, just Michael. Father's such a High Anglican thing. We like to keep things a little less formal in Tollinghill.'

'Got any digestives?' Ellis Flint asked; always keen to fuel his body wherever possible in order to avoid the culinary nightmares that Mrs Flint tended to concoct for his meal each evening.

'It's a terrible business, this murder,' the vicar said as he handed Ellis a packet of biscuits and placed the porcelain lid back on the teapot, thoughts of pigs going through Flint's mind.

'Yes, it's rarely jolly,' Hardwick replied, with more than a hint of sarcasm.

'"Therefore we are always confident and know that as long as we are at home in the body we are away from the Lord. For we live by faith, not by sight. We are confident, I say, and would prefer to be away from the body and at home with the Lord." 2 Corinthians 5:6-8.' The vicar smiled and handed Hardwick his cup of tea.

'Indeed,' Hardwick replied. 'Although may I say I find it a little callous to suggest that Oscar Whitehouse wanted to be murdered?'

'Oh, I'm not suggesting that for one moment. The quote is intended to give comfort that Oscar is now at peace and at one — at home — with the Lord,' replied the vicar.

'Well I'm sure he'd rather be at home with his family, personally, but I'm sure we can agree to disagree.'

'So!' Ellis Flint interjected, sensing the deepening atmosphere. 'Lovely day, isn't it?'

'No,' Hardwick said.

'Raining,' the vicar added.

'It's only a small shower, I'm sure,' said Ellis. 'The reason we wanted to speak to you, vicar, is that Kempston and I–' he said, emphasising his name in order to break the death stare between Hardwick and the reverend. 'Well, we were speaking to a few of the witnesses from last night and it seems that you were in the room from the time that Oscar Whitehouse's body was discovered, until the point that the police arrived.'

'Well,' the vicar said, visibly trying to remember. 'I think you may be right, yes.'

'Does that not strike you as a little suspicious, sir?' Hardwick asked.

'Well why should it? He was dead before I even got there. Why should it matter how long I spent in the company of a dead body? I spend half of my life in the company of dead bodies.'

'And the other half praying to one,' Hardwick muttered under his breath.

'Was anything moved or altered between finding Oscar Whitehouse's body and the police arriving?' Ellis asked.

'Nothing, other than moving his body slightly, to

check he was dead. I explicitly stayed in the room in order to provide continuity and ensure everything was preserved.'

The vicar's version of events thereafter ran much the same as those of the other partygoers, so Hardwick and Flint saw little reason to drag the conversation out for any longer than they needed to. Ellis Flint, in particular, was keen to put an end to the tense atmosphere between the vicar and Hardwick.

During his formative years, Hardwick had spent most of his time travelling around the world as his parents' work took them from continent to continent. Having lived in places as diverse as Patagonia, Russia and the Horn of Africa, he had come to realise that although the concept and details of religion differed vastly between cultures and regions, its divisive nature and sense of self-importance often seemed to permeate all that was good about their individual message.

'I thought you were a little harsh on him there, Kempston,' Flint said as they left the vicarage.

'Not especially, Ellis. I can't stand all the religious hokum.'

'I know, I've noticed. But it hardly has any impact on our investigation, does it? A little respect for the man's beliefs wouldn't go amiss.'

'On the contrary, Ellis. Detection and religion

cannot possibly go hand in hand. They are two opposite sides of the same coin: one uses its head and the other relies on tales.' As he spoke, he spotted the figure of a Mediterranean man—whom he presumed to be Christos Karagounis—walking past the vicarage wall. 'Excuse me? Mr Karagounis? I'm Kempston Hardwick, and this is Ellis Flint. Can we have a quick word, please?'

Christos Karagounis was an odd-looking man, much like a cartoonist or TV impressionist might make a Greek Cypriot out to be; his well-slicked hair clung to his ears in a seemingly random manner, yet unwavering in the Saturday morning breeze. He wore a short-sleeved button-up shirt with a horrendous flowered pattern, and looked as though he were about to die from heat exhaustion.

'Like I tell police, Mr Hardwick. I not particularly surprised,' Christos Karagounis said, in a heavy accent laden with a surprising contrast of simple grammatical errors yet impressively advanced vocabulary.

'And why would that be, Mr Karagounis?' Ellis Flint asked, his youthful exuberance belying his forty-some-thing years.

'He have many enemies. In this line of work, he have many people who see him as charlatan and fraudster.'

'I see. And where were you last night?'

'I was at home, in my cottage. I was browsing

internet and on telephone to my mother. All night. You can see internet log and phone record,' Christos said, insistently.

'I'm sure there's no need. Tell me, how long have you lived in England, Mr Karagounis?' Hardwick asked, desperate to uncover the riddle of the gardener's topsy-turvy grasp of the language.

'Five years this autumn. Why you ask?'

'Pure curiosity,' Hardwick replied. 'I assure you.'

Christos Karagounis seemed placated for the moment.

'Do you have much need for advanced English in your work?' Hardwick asked of the gardener.

'Not especially, no. Of course, I need speak with Mr and Mrs Whitehouse, but in Shafford we have very vibrant Greek community. Many restaurant and social club.'

Hardwick, being an extremely well-travelled man and an especial fan of Mediterranean cuisine, knew of Shafford's Greek restaurants all too well.

'Tell me, Κος Καραγκούνης,' Hardwick offered, in Greek, in an attempt to endear himself to the gardener. 'Did Oscar and Eliza Whitehouse often argue?'

'Oh, my, my, yes!' Christos Karagounis replied, his wonderfully Mediterranean gesticulation making Hardwick feel slightly sea-sick, although the gardener did seem to have gained a new level of trust and confidence. 'Mr and Mrs Whitehouse have many volatile argument.'

'Over what,' Ellis Flint asked. 'Do you know?'

The gardener chuckled a little and leaned in to Hardwick and Flint, as if telling them a cheeky secret. 'Let me say, Mr Whitehouse have trouble keeping at bay the little panty lizard!'

Ellis Flint's eyebrows rose like rockets as he looked at Hardwick, trying to work out what on earth Christos Karagounis was talking about. Without missing a beat, Hardwick wrapped up the conversation and bade the gardener farewell. 'And please don't go anywhere in the next few days,' he added. 'We may just need to speak to you again.'

'What the hell...?' Flint asked as he and Hardwick reached the car, which was parked at the side of the road. 'Panty lizard?'

'Oh, Ellis. Your knowledge of colloquial idioms fails you. Trouser snake, Ellis. Trouser snake. You really do surprise me sometimes.'

Ellis stood, dumbfounded, as Hardwick climbed into the driver's seat.

'You and me both, Hardwick. You and me both.'

13

'Thank you for taking the time to speak to us, Dr Daniels,' Hardwick said, his eyes glancing around the kitchen of the modest semi-detached house. 'I understand you were the locum doctor working in and around Tollinghill last night.'

'That's right, yes. Would either of you like coffee? Tea?'

'No, thank you.'

'Tea, please,' Ellis Flint replied.

'Sugar?'

'Six, please.'

'Dr Daniels, I'll cut to the chase,' Hardwick said, in a rare display of the vernacular. 'A patient of yours died a few hours after your visit on Friday night.'

The doctor put the kettle down on the work surface

with a start and palmed his forehead. 'Oh dear, oh dear. I knew it. I could see it coming a mile off. Oh, God! Why didn't I say something at the time?'

'What, Dr Daniels? What is it?'

'I should have just dislodged the Lego brick myself; not sent her to A&E! Oh, God, I'm such an idiot!'

'Sorry, Lego brick?' Hardwick asked.

Dr Daniels stopped hyperventilating for a moment. 'You are here about Mrs Yardley, aren't you?'

'No, Dr Daniels. We're here about Oscar Whitehouse.'

Dr Daniels was visibly calmed. 'Oh! Well, that is a relief. Well, not a relief. Dead? He only had a virus! At least I think he did... Oh, God! I got it wrong, didn't I?'

'Oh, it wasn't the virus that killed him. He was strangled.'

'Christ... And you think I did it? Oh, God!'

'Dr Daniels, will you pull yourself together? Oscar Whitehouse was seen alive a number of times after your visit. We're here because we're speaking to everyone who saw him on Friday night. Now, why were you called to Westerlea House that night?'

'The call came from his wife, I think. I was the on-duty locum so I went out and saw him. He was in bed when I got there. Very pale, cold sweats, some vomiting and diarrhoea. Nothing of any major concern — just another case of influenza or rhinovirus. There's plenty of it going around.'

'And what did you prescribe?'

'For a virus? There's nothing you can prescribe. Except sleep, orange juice and chicken soup.'

'And how was his wife throughout all of this?'

'She seemed quite worried at first, but calmed down fairly quickly. I seem to recall she said something about a party that night. I told her that she needn't alter any plans and that Mr Whitehouse would be absolutely fine. Mostly out of action, but fine.'

'And you noticed nothing else of any suspicion?'

'Nothing at all, no. How on earth was he murdered in the middle of a party? Surely that's impossible!' the doctor said.

'Not especially. There weren't all that many people there — only a small handful of friends and neighbours. That will have made the killer's job somewhat easier,' Hardwick replied.

'And do you think it was one of the partygoers who killed him?'

'So it would seem.'

14

Much of detective work, it seemed to Hardwick, was rather puerile, consisting mostly of ping-ponging back and forth between witnesses, family and friends in a rather crass and insensitive manner – even for Hardwick. So it was that they found themselves once again at Westerlea House, this time in the garden, barely a handful of hours after they had last left it.

The dawn of a new day could make or break an investigation, and this Saturday afternoon visit would yield the answer as to whether this particular investigation would be made or broken. The fresh rising sun could often cajole a person into revealing new details and subconsciously help to unravel a whole mystery. Conversely, it could provide ample time for a guilty party to take heed and shore up one's defences.

Eliza Whitehouse seemed neither defensive nor enlightened that afternoon, instead she had the air of a woman who had rather abruptly come to terms with her bereavement and was intent on dealing with it in a calm, organised and orderly manner.

The tea was poured, and the biscuits served, so Eliza Whitehouse set her stall for a chat with Hardwick and Flint.

Hardwick spoke first. 'How long has your gardener, Mr Karagounis, been working for you, Mrs Whitehouse?'

'Christos?' she asked, stirring a spoonful of sugar into her china cup. 'Oh, almost four years now I suppose. Yes, we first hired him after we'd returned from our trip to Canada. It's a terribly big garden for a practically retired couple to look after, you know, and a six-week break in the height of summer leaves one's lawns and flowerbeds in a terrible state. We just didn't have the heart to even know where to begin. That's when we hired Christos to get on top of things. He did such a good job; we've kept him on ever since.'

'Would you say Mr Karagounis is a trustworthy character, Mrs Whitehouse?' Ellis Flint asked, getting characteristically to the point.

'Oh, yes, absolutely. He can do wonders with a

rhododendron, you know. You should see the way he manipulates my clematis!' Eliza Whitehouse began to fan herself with a nearby leaflet, because, Hardwick hoped, of the heat and humidity of the day.

Ellis spluttered into the cup of tea which was raised to his lips. He apologised profusely and delicately wiped a small brown stain from Eliza Whitehouse's blouse.

Hardwick took up the reins. 'Mrs Whitehouse, your gardener mentioned that perhaps your marriage was... well, let's say interesting.'

'Well,' Eliza said, straightening her shoulders and wriggling in the wicker garden chair, 'I think it's safe to say that most marriages go through one or two rough patches. You must know that yourself.'

'I'm afraid not,' Hardwick said, shaking his head. 'Life's too short to be shared, if you ask me, Mrs White-house. Now, Mr Karagounis did mention the possibility of the occasional... altercation, regarding... well, fidelity.'

'I beg your pardon?' Eliza responded, as she immediately stopped fanning herself.

Ellis Flint was used to having to be a human thesaurus in order to decode Hardwick's roundabout way of getting, eventually (when all was said and done), to the – let's say – final point. 'He mentioned your husband's trou–'

Hardwick coughed rather loudly and abruptly, 'Trout! Trout... recipes,' he said, glaring at Flint. 'He mentioned that your husband had a rather good trout recipe.'

'No...' Eliza replied, now rather confused. 'I don't recall Oscar ever having cooked in all the time we were married. He certainly wasn't a fan of fish, anyway.'

'Ah,' Hardwick said, once again being forced to think on his feet, whilst placating a live-wire Ellis Flint. 'Well, a matter of opinion, perhaps. I tend to find it has a rather good taste, don't you, Ellis? I find fish to be rather sensitive. A rather dignified food.'

By now, even Ellis had cottoned on to Hardwick's not-so-hidden meaning.

'Oh yes, absolutely. Fish are very caring, aren't they, Kempston?'

'Caring? Fish?' Eliza Whitehouse asked. Hardwick cursed quietly to himself.

'Oh, for... Mrs Whitehouse,' Hardwick said, staring daggers at Ellis Flint. 'I hate to ask this, but do you know if your husband had ever been unfaithful to you?'

Eliza was silent for a few moments, before calmly saying, 'Who told you that?'

'Mrs Whitehouse, we just need to find out whether _'

'Who told you?' she asked again, this time more forcefully.

'Mr Karagounis simply mentioned that –'

'Oh, yes, I thought he might! Bloody meddling man...'

'What sort of relationship did your husband have with Sandy Baker, may I ask?'

Eliza Whitehouse made a noise reminiscent of a Morris Minor failing to start on a cold January morning. 'Who knows? If you ask me, they were having it off left, right and centre.'

Hardwick shuffled slightly on his chair, as if swayed by a strong breeze. 'What... what do you mean, exactly? You have proof that they were having an affair?'

'Oh, not proof, exactly. It's very difficult to get proof of something like that, other than having him come out and tell me. As a persistent liar, that was never particularly likely. No, call it a woman's intuition if you will. You get to learn the little signs.'

'So you suspected that he'd been wandering in the past, too?' Hardwick asked.

'Oh God, yes. I've no proof that he and Sandy had anything going on, but if you stack up all the women and all the pieces of circumstantial evidence over the years, then I'm sure it would look pretty conclusive. He revelled in playing with women, you see. Stupid old sod couldn't even see that they were only interested in him for the money and fame.'

'Do you think it's possible that one of these women might be in some way responsible for your husband's death?'

'I wouldn't be at all surprised,' Eliza replied. 'But I couldn't even begin to tell you who any of them were.'

15

The bells that rang out across Tollinghill to alert the congregation to the sole service at eleven o'clock that Sunday morning seemed somewhat more maudlin than usual. Harry Greenlaw, who was handing out leaflets at the front door, noted that more than a few unfamiliar faces had come along to that particular Sunday service. It was at the most tragic and uncertain of times, he realised, that lapsed Christians tended to flock to church.

Although the numbers were larger than for most sermons, Reverend Michael noted that the murmurings from the congregation were far more muted than on quieter weeks. Word of a tragedy moves far more quickly than that of God's good news, he observed, without much surprise. This service, however, was to be a very different one. It had a more funereal feel than those to which the parishioners were usually accustomed, with the traditional format being abandoned.

'"Whoever sheds the blood of man, by man shall his blood be shed, for God made man in his own image." The words of God to Noah. Genesis 9:6,' Reverend Michael opened.

'This is not an easy sermon for me to have to deliver. I deal with the circle of life on a daily basis as part of my work for our Lord God, but I have that same good Lord to thank for the rarity of having to experience the blood of man shed by man himself. Murder,' he emphasised, 'is thankfully rare. To have such a crime committed on our own doorstep — a doorstep which I myself had crossed that very evening — is unspeakable. But speak about it we must, as an evil force is amongst us today in Tollinghill.

'Thou shalt not murder is one of the cornerstones of the Ten Commandments. The one commandment, perhaps, which no amount of social modernity and liberalisation will change. Someone amongst us certainly did not observe the commandment to love thy neighbour. The Ten Commandments also tell us that we must not bear false witness. Proverbs 6:16-19 tells us "There are six things that the Lord strongly dislikes, seven that are an abomination to him: haughty eyes, a lying tongue, hands that shed innocent blood, a heart that devises wicked plans, feet that make haste to run to evil, a false witness who breathes out lies, and one who sows discord among brothers.'"

Reverend Michael continued with his sermon for a further fifteen minutes, reeling off a selection of carefully chosen Bible verses and implored a level of soul searching amongst the residents of Tollinghill. Having stated that no hymns would be sung at that particular service, he led the congregation in prayer for the safe passage of the soul of Oscar Whitehouse, strength and courage for his family and peace and integrity for the person responsible.

Kempston Hardwick, not being one who made a habit of attending church services, had relied on Ellis Flint to survey the scene. Quite how he was supposed to gauge the reactions of certain parishioners and the effect of the words of the Reverend Michael Winton when he had sat himself down at the very back of the church was anyone's guess, but Ellis took on his new role of detectivial independence with great fervour. Having satisfied himself that, unsurprisingly, there were no signs of suspicion, he rose during the last prayer and headed for the sanctity and solitude of the Freemason's Arms.

16

The usual Sunday-lunchtime clientele were assembled in the Freemason's Arms as Ellis Flint pushed open the large door and sat himself down on the nearest barstool. Four gentlemen of advancing years were spaced out neatly along the length of the bar, so Ellis chose to complete the pattern by propping against at the adjacent stretch of the L-shaped bar.

'Ol' Terrence here tells me you were in church today, Ellis. I 'ope you're not goin' soft on us,' Doug Lilley, the long-standing landlord said, as he poured his fifth customer a pint.

Bearing in mind that he had snuck out early and was a good thirty years younger than Terrence (he never knew his surname and didn't care to find out), Ellis was stunned that the man had managed to get to the pub before him.

'Nah, probably feeling guilty, ain't he?' Terrence replied before Ellis could think of what to say. 'Probably bumped off that Whitehouse bloke!'

Ellis was again stunned into silence, but thankfully saved by Doug. 'Not bloody likely, Terrence. It's 'im wot's been tryin' to find out who done it!'

'I know,' Terrence said, in the manner of a child having been reprimanded by its parent. 'Only messing, like. No offence, Ellis.'

'None taken.'

'Just meant that everyone's a suspect, ain't they? Never know who done it. Could be any one, really. Ain't that right, Doug?'

'Right,' Doug replied, 'but that don't mean you need to go around shootin' your mouth off accusin' people of murder. We got to all rally round, aven't we? I tell you what, Ellis: when you find out who done that to ol' Oscar, I've got a right mind to go round there 'n wring 'is bloody neck!'

Ellis tried to diffuse the situation, but not before a long, cool draught of his beer to counteract the effects of the warm summer's walk from the church.

'Not much point in that, is there? Letting him get

away scot-free then. Better to let him rot in jail, surely?'
Ellis said — very diplomatically, he thought.

The landlord cocked his head to his side and curled
his bottom lip forward. 'True. Fair point, I s'pose.' Before
he could say any more, the front door to the pub swung
open and the familiar figure of Kempston Hardwick
entered and made a beeline for Ellis.

'Well?'

'Well what?' Ellis asked.

'What happened at the church service? Did you spot
anything unusual?'

'Only the fact that I was sat in a church on a Sunday
morning. Do you want a drink?'

'No, Ellis, I want to know all about the church
service.'

'Well you should've come along then, shouldn't you?
Lovely, it was. Really strong moral message. I'm having a
beer if you want one.'

'Oh, for... All right, I'll have a Campari. But then I
want to hear every last detail.'

'All out, I'm afraid,' Doug said from behind the bar,
having not-so-subtly listened in on their conversation.
'You drank the last drop.'

'A half of whatever Ellis is having, then,' Hardwick
said, before turning back to Flint. 'Let's get a table over
there in the corner.'

'I thought you preferred sitting at the bar?' Ellis said, his eyes narrowing.

'I do,' he said, glancing at the landlord, 'but I think this particular conversation needs a little more privacy.'

With the drinks poured and paid for, the pair made their way over to the corner table and sat down, Hardwick opting for the large green cloth armchair, which sat regally under a glowing lampshade in the far corner of the pub. Ellis was right — Hardwick did tend to prefer sitting at the bar, but he couldn't help but secure that particular chair whenever it was available.

'Now, run me through what happened,' Hardwick said, taking a sip of his beer and licking the line of white foam from his upper lip.

'Not a whole lot, if I'm honest. I mean, I don't go to church often, but weddings and funerals tend to be a lot more eventful than that.'

'Yes, that's why they're called "events", Ellis. The clue's in the name. Did you get a good look at our main suspects? Did anyone seem a little... suspicious? Keen, perhaps. Or unduly nervous?'

'Difficult to say, really. I couldn't see everyone's faces the whole time. I wasn't in what you might call a prime viewing position.'

'Why? Where did you sit?'

'At the back.'

'At the back? Jesus Christ, man. How did you expect to see anything at the back?'

'I could see the vicar perfectly well. He's a suspect. Besides, he'd not be keen on you taking the good Lord's name in vain.'

'Ellis,' Hardwick said, with a long sigh. 'I'm investigating a murder case. I think even the good Lord would permit me the occasional oral misdemeanour.'

The elderly woman who happened to be walking past their table at that moment picked the remains of her sherry glass out of the carpet and made her way back to the bar, casting the occasional revolted glance at Hardwick. 'I thought that lot kept themselves away down in Brighton,' she said, as she ordered a replacement drink.

'What was the service like?' Hardwick asked Flint.

'Odd.'

'Odd?'

'Yeah, odd. No hymns, for a start. Quite a solemn affair, really. Bit like a funeral but without the songs or the hysterical relatives. He seemed quite stern. As if he knew that the murderer was there, in the pews.'

'You mean he knew they were there somewhere, or you think he actually knew who it was?' Hardwick asked, his interest piqued.

'Difficult to say, really,' Ellis said, taking a sip of his drink. 'But I think we can safely say he knows more than he's letting on.'

17

Having spent the previous afternoon and evening clearing his mind from distractions, Hardwick had been pleasantly surprised to discover that Oscar Whitehouse's agent and PR representative, Sandy Baker, was in the office bright and early the next morning.

'I know it's early for a Monday, but Sandy and the directors wanted to meet as early as possible to discuss what to do after Friday night,' the young receptionist had explained. 'Not the sort of thing we get very often. I mean, clients die, but we've never had one murdered,' she added with protruding eyeballs. 'I'll call her for you.'

'Thank you. Much obliged,' Hardwick said as he and Flint sat down on a plush purple sofa in the reception area. A selection of upmarket interior design magazines adorned the low solid-glass coffee table.

The layout and design of contemporary offices was yet another aspect of the modern world that Hardwick couldn't quite get his head around. There seemed to be no walls; just panes of frosted glass jutting out left, right and centre. Frosted, Hardwick presumed, to avoid major injury.

'Sorry to bother you, Sandy,' the young girl said into her headset, 'but the police are here to talk about Friday night.'

'Oh! No, we're not–' Flint started.

'Not in any rush,' Hardwick interrupted, glaring at Flint. 'She's more than welcome to take her time.'

Barely moments later, the slim, blonde figure of Sandy Baker body-swerved a pane of frosted glass and flounced through into the reception area, introducing herself.

'Follow me; we'll chat in my office,' she added.

Sandy Baker's office was of a contemporary design, with a number of completely irrelevant decorations and ornaments. Her desk backed onto a window with a view over the town and faced an open lounge-like area, which consisted of two brightly-coloured egg-pod-style chairs and a beanbag.

Guiding the pair to this side of the office, Sandy sat

herself down in one of the egg pods and motioned for Ellis to take the other. Unsure as to how exactly to sit in it, Ellis tried both leg-first and head-first before opting for the spiralling cat manoeuvre. Finally he found a position that left him comfortable enough, but looking rather like a coy geisha. Hardwick, on the other hand, was left with the beanbag and chose to stand.

'Please, sit down,' Sandy offered.

'I'm quite all right standing, Ms Baker,' Hardwick said.

'Nonsense. We go for the relaxed feeling in this office. Please sit down,' she implored.

Hardwick stood for a moment and looked askance at Ellis Flint. Seeing the blatant awkwardness of the seating arrangements, but not considering for one second that he could look half as daft as Flint, he slowly lowered himself towards the beanbag, his right arm out behind to support him.

After he had righted himself, rubbed his bruised elbow and extracted his pen from his earhole, Hardwick asked Sandy about her visit to Westerlea House on Friday night.

'Yes, I went over at about... let's see. I left the office at eight-thirty, so probably about nine o'clock? I wanted to see how he was and take him some paperwork to sign. It needed to be filed by Saturday morning so unfortunately I had no choice.'

'How long did you stay for?' Ellis asked.

'Oh, not long. Five minutes at the most.'

'And what was this paperwork, exactly?' Hardwick enquired.

'Just various bits and bobs, really.'

'It can't have been that important then, surely?' Hardwick said, cocking his head to one side.

'Well, one piece was a contract for a new show on one of the paranormal channels. They wanted him to go round to other people's houses and speak to the ghosts that haunted them.'

'And that contract was the piece that needed to be signed by Saturday morning?'

'Yes, otherwise the show wouldn't have gone ahead and we would have lost the money.'

'I see. May I take a copy of the contract with me?'

'Yes, of course,' Sandy said, standing from her egg pod and rifling through a stack of papers on her desk. 'Ah, here it is. I'll get the receptionist to photocopy it for you.'

'Thank you. Now tell me, what was your relationship with Oscar Whitehouse like?'

'Oh, very positive,' Sandy said, sitting at her desk chair. Hardwick noted that she no longer felt the need for a casual egg-based approach. 'He always put on a good performance and was sought after by lots of different television shows. He was always professional in his work and was one of our stars.'

'I mean your personal relationship,' Hardwick explained.

'Ah. Well that was fine, too.'

'Fine?'

Sandy thought for a few moments and sighed. 'He was a good client but not a particularly pleasant man.'

Hardwick raised an eyebrow, signalling that she should continue.

'He was very demanding. None of this came across on camera, of course, which is why he was so popular with audiences and producers. He always pulled in the viewers and his books sold by the bucket load, which suited us down to the ground. On a personal level, though, he was very rude and arrogant. He had a bit of a reputation with women, if you want to know the truth.'

'In what sense?' Hardwick asked.

'Well he was very flirtatious. He was part of the old-school; he thought he could have any woman he wanted just because he was on television. He liked to try it on and wouldn't take no for an answer. But then again, like I say, he came from that sort of background. It was rife in the seventies and eighties — I think everyone knows that by now.'

'Perhaps so,' Hardwick said, 'but that doesn't make it right.'

'No, of course it doesn't, but it does explain it.'

Hardwick was silent for a few moments, allowing Sandy Baker to judge her own remarks without any comment of his own.

'Did he ever "try it on" with you, Ms Baker?'

Sandy glanced down at her desk, as if the answer lay there. 'There may have been one or two situations, but I don't let things like that get in the way of a good business relationship,' Sandy said, her cracking voice belying her words.

'I apologise, but I really do need to ask,' Hardwick explained. 'Did he ever assault you?'

'Right,' Sandy said, removing herself from her chair. 'Is that the time? Sorry, I have another meeting to get to. If you need anything else, please do call or email me.'

Hardwick held the photocopied contract in his hand and was silent for almost a full minute.

'You've got an idea, haven't you, Kempston?' Ellis said.

'Perhaps. This contract bound Oscar Whitehouse to a new television series, yes?'

'Apparently so, yes,' Ellis replied.

'A television series that he could never actually work on, seeing as he died the same night as he signed the contract.'

'Well, it would have been pretty tricky if you ask me, yes.'

'I wonder... Ellis, come with me. We're going to see an old friend.'

18

The office that Hardwick led Flint into was far more traditional and less ostentatious than the one Sandy Baker operated from. The wood panelling on the walls in the waiting area (sans receptionist) looked as though it could tell a thousand stories from a million overheard conversations. A few minutes after their arrival, the door to the office opened and a tall, gaunt-looking man greeted Hardwick.

'Kempston! Well, what a wonderful surprise. Do come in, the two of you.'

As the man closed the door behind them, Hardwick saw fit to introduce Ellis.

'Solly, this is Ellis Flint, a friend and colleague of mine. Ellis, this is Solly Abrahams — he's a solicitor.'

The two men exchanged handshakes and pleas-antries and sat down at the desk.

'I presume this isn't a social visit, Kempston?' Solly asked.

'Indeed not. I need you to take a look at a contract for me. It's to do with a case I'm working on. It's a contract for a new television show, which Oscar White-house was meant to present and star in.'

'Ah. And now he's dead. Yes, I saw it in the news-paper this morning. Terrible business.'

'Indeed. Interestingly, the contract was signed by Oscar Whitehouse on the same night as he died. What does that mean in legal terms?'

'Well, I think it's safe to say that one can only presume he signed it before he died. In which case, the document became legally binding straight away. It depends on who had a stake in Oscar Whitehouse's career, really. I presume that, like most television person-alities, he must have had an agent or management company of some sort. They usually cream a large percentage from any earnings. Seeing as they had a stake in the value of this contract, and old Oscar then went and died before it could be fulfilled, it's likely the insur-ance would pay out. That's if his death was no fault of his own, of course, by which I mean, as long as he didn't commit suicide.'

'He didn't. Pay out to whom?' Hardwick asked.

'Whoever held the policy; I should imagine it would be his agent or management company. They fulfilled their side of the contract and were due to earn a decent amount of money. Circumstances robbed them of that, so any insurance policy would cover them for loss of earnings.'

Hardwick thought for a few moments, rubbing his chin. 'So let's get this straight. Oscar Whitehouse's agent — or management company — would be due a big insurance pay-out if he died before the programme was completed?'

'That's about the long and short of it, yes.'

19

There were very few people that Hardwick would tolerate an unannounced visit from early on a Monday morning, and members of the local clergy were usually not included.

Hardwick said nothing as he opened the door, instead raising one eyebrow whilst he waited for his unannounced visitor to announce himself.

'I'm terribly sorry to bother you,' Reverend Michael Winton started, 'but I really do need to talk to you.'

Hardwick sighed and stepped aside to let the vicar through into the hallway. Once they had settled in the living room (drinks offered but declined), the vicar shuffled nervously and looked around. His eyes rested on a mahogany trinket box, which sat on the bookcase in front of a selection of Jules Verne tomes.

'That's a beautiful item you have there. What is it?'

'It's a box, vicar,' Hardwick replied bluntly.

'I see. It looks South American to me. Is it?'

'It is indeed. Patagonian. The Aysén region.'

'Ah. Is that the Argentinian half or the Chilean?'

Hardwick stared at the reverend for a few moments before answering. 'Chilean, naturally.'

'Well, it's beautiful. When were you over there?'

'When I was younger, mostly.' Hardwick was not one to talk about his past, but (even though non-religious) he found himself quite comfortable talking to the vicar. 'My father was an environmental scientist; a leader in his field. We travelled around a lot.'

'Mostly South America, was it?'

'Not at all. I also spent a lot of time in Scandinavia, India, New Zealand and the Far East. Oh, and quite a few years in and around sub-Saharan Africa.'

'A very well-travelled man, then!'

'A man without a home, vicar,' Hardwick said as he smiled.

'Every man has a home, Kempston, which brings me to my point. I'm not sure how involved you are in the church, you see, but my role as priest isn't just that of preaching the faith, but also that of a community leader. A friend, if you like. Quite often local parishioners will come to me and want to speak about issues in their lives.

I suppose it's a kind of confidence issue. In this day and age, the vicar's about the only person you can trust. It's quite encouraging, really, that in the modern age religion is still—'

'Fascinating, vicar,' Hardwick began, as he rose to his feet, 'but time really is getting on.'

'No, no,' the reverend continued, 'that's not all. You see, I really have to get something off my chest... Oh, Lord please forgive me. I shouldn't even be telling you this, you see –'

'You've told me very little so far, vicar, believe me,' Hardwick said.

'Yes, well... you see, I was told one or two things which I think might just have a bearing on the murder of Oscar Whitehouse.'

Hardwick sat down again very quickly.

'You have to understand me when I say the word of God is a powerful one, and that I cannot divulge any information that I've been told, but the weight of this is killing me, Mr Hardwick.'

'The weight of what, vicar?'

'What I've been told!'

'Yes, I appreciate that. But without knowing what you've been told, there's very little I can do about it.'

'That's just the problem. I could not possibly divulge anything that I'm made privy to in confidence. You see, there's a distinct difference between the Roman Catholic idea of reconciliation and the Church of England's approach to confession. Roman Catholics, amongst other remarkable things,' the vicar said, with a slight hint of sarcasm, 'believe that the confessional allows them to be absolved of their sins purely by admitting to them. Now, we on this side of the river know that's barking mad, but it doesn't make what's said in confidence any less confidential. We believe in the trust of God, and that must be adhered to, lest we commit a crime far worse than the confessor.'

'Worse than murder?' Hardwick barked incredulously, momentarily stunning the vicar. Hardwick was not known for his bursts of anger, but even the most mild-mannered of men are prone to the odd outburst at times of extreme frustration. 'You really don't get it, do you? A man has died! A family has been left without its father; its husband; its son. You are the one person who has knowledge of something that might just be able to help find his killer and you put the sanctity of a mythical God before the law of this country? Are you mad, man?'

'The law of this country is based on the laws and teachings of God, Mr Hardwick,' the vicar tried to explain calmly, his hands visibly shaking with poorly-hidden anger.

'For crying out loud, vicar! There is no God!'

The reverend stood and said nothing. Only the slightest flicker of his eyes and the clenching of his fists and teeth betrayed his inner fury.

'Good night, Hardwick,' he managed, somehow remaining calm and composed as he walked to the door, opened it and closed it softly behind him.

20

The sun began to break through the clouds late on Monday afternoon as Hardwick and Flint left the Old Rectory and made their way slowly towards Westerlea House. Hardwick mulled over the vicar's words on everybody having a natural home, as he admired the gently swaying wisteria and listened to the rising birdsong.

'Must be quite odd for you, Kempston, living in what used to be the rectory.'

'Not especially,' Hardwick replied, smiling inwardly at the sight of the local village postman cycling past the duck pond.

'How did that happen, anyway? Two rectories and all that. Surely you have one rectory per church?'

'You do, yes. Did you not study the dissolution of the monasteries at school, Ellis?'

'Yes, but I didn't tend to listen much.'

'Well, old habits die hard, eh, Ellis? My house used to be the rectory for the original church at Tollinghill. The church was destroyed during the dissolution but the rectory remained. When the newer Church of England church was built, they decided to build it on the site where it stands to this day. Thereby leaving me, and generations before me, with a very nice house indeed. Say what you like about Henry VIII, but I quite like the chap.'

'That means your place must be almost five-hundred years old!' Ellis replied. 'Blimey. And it's still three times the size of the "new" vicarage.'

'Yes, well the Catholic Church had the backing of a few Medici Popes during the sixteenth century, who tended to keep the whole system rather flush with cash. Blood money, some might say. The Medici family practically invented banking, so it's hardly surprising that they became rather wealthy. They were the first real gangsters, the Medici. You can draw the bloodline right through to some particular families living in Sicily to this day. Make of that what you will, Ellis. The Church of England, however, wasn't quite so financially blessed in its formative years.'

They walked in silence for a few moments before Ellis decided to broach a subject that he'd been dying to bring up for a long time.

'What do you have against the Church, exactly, Kempston?'

'Me? Nothing in particular. Why do you ask?'

'Just a few things I've noticed – reactions and things you've said. All that stuff about the mafia and blood money. Besides, you weren't exactly pleasant to Michael Winton this morning from what I've heard.'

'Please don't mention that man's name, Ellis.'

'See what I mean? It's hardly fair, Kempston.'

'No, Ellis,' Hardwick barked, stopping in his tracks. 'What's not fair is withholding evidence that could lead to the identification and capture of a killer.' Ellis looked bemusedly at Hardwick, who continued. 'The vicar came to see me earlier. The whole conversation was quite futile and hugely frustrating. He told me that he has been told something in confession, which has a bearing on the case in hand. Of course, he couldn't bloody tell me anyway because of his duties to the Church, so it was completely pointless him coming to see me in the first place. I really don't know what he hoped to gain, but it's made me very angry.'

'So I can see,' Ellis replied. 'I thought confessionals were a Catholic thing, though?'

'In a sense, they are. Church of England vicars accept confession, but it's more of a confidential chat than anything structured. No immediate absolution of sin or any of that nonsense. Still, it's a spanner in the works because the level of confidence still applies.'

'Surely if a priest or vicar is party to information on an illegal activity, he could be prosecuted for perverting the course of justice!'

'That all depends, Ellis. I did a bit of research this morning as I'm not exactly au fait with clerical matters. Church of England legislation says, "There can be no disclosure of what is confessed to a priest. This principle holds even after the death of the penitent. The priest may not refer to what has been learnt in confession, even to the penitent, unless explicitly permitted." By the same token, it says, "If a penitent's behaviour gravely threatens his or her well-being or that of others, the priest, while advising action on the penitent's part, must still keep the confidence."'

'How on earth did you remember all that?'

'It's a case of having to.'

'It makes no sense, though. Surely if the vicar was made party to something connected with a murder then he'd have to tell the police!'

'Yes, I'd imagine so. Michael Winton strikes me as the sort of person who'd do the right thing. But for all we

know, what he was told could be something quite innocent in itself, but forms a vital clue in the investigation.
Either way, it's damned frustrating, Ellis. I do, however,
have some good news.'

'Go on...' Ellis enquired.

'In preparation for our visit to Andrew Whitehouse
this afternoon, I did a little bit of research into Oscar and
Eliza's little philosophical prodigy. It seems he's not
quite as clean-cut as it may appear.'

'Nobody's ever clean-cut at university, Kempston.'

'Quite, but even your average university student
would stop short of hospitalising a taxi driver, Ellis.'

'Christ. When was this?'

'Eighteen months ago. It wasn't difficult to find: it
made the inside columns of a few red-tops owing to the
celebrity status of his father, but never made front-page
news. It seems the university swept it under the carpet
somewhat, too.'

'What happened?' Ellis asked.

'Judging purely on the newspaper reports, Andrew
Whitehouse got into a heated argument with a taxi
driver over the cost of a fare, and that somehow resulted
in the driver having to have a metal plate fitted in his
skull.'

'Wow. That's quite an argument.'

'Indeed. Not only was the taxi driver lucky to make

a quick recovery, but Andrew Whitehouse was fortunate enough to escape with a community order. The judge recognised that his behaviour was usually impeccable and that alcohol played a large part. Either way, it's proof that his behaviour in certain situations can be volatile to the point of being dangerous.'

'And he was drinking at the party! What's to say he didn't go upstairs and kill his father?'

'One step at a time, Ellis,' Hardwick said as pair finally reached the front gates to Westerlea House. 'Let's speak to him first and see what he has to say for himself.'

'Mum's out at her sister's,' Andrew Whitehouse said as he opened the front door. 'She should be back later this evening.'

'That's quite all right. It's you we wanted to speak to, actually,' Ellis said.

Andrew Whitehouse said nothing, but stepped aside and let Hardwick and Flint enter the house, which was starting to become more than a little familiar to them. No matter how many times they came here, Ellis never failed to be awestruck by the fantastic hallway onto which the front door opened. A large open staircase spiralled ninety degrees from the right-hand wall, up and across the rear of the house, exposing the long landing and bedroom doors.

As the whole of the upstairs landing was open plan and covered three walls of the building, Ellis had previously registered the immense difficulty with which a potential murderer could have entered and left Oscar Whitehouse's bedroom unseen – especially in the midst of a party – and the puzzle struck him again as he stood inside the house.

The ground floor of Westerlea House followed much the same floor plan, with the dining room to the left, living room to the right and a large kitchen and separate utility room to the rear of the house. Hardwick and Flint were ushered into the living room.

'We just want to ask you a few questions, if we may,' Hardwick began.

'Routine stuff, I'm sure you understand,' Flint added.

'Yes, thank you, Ellis. Now, what sort of a relationship did you have with your father?'

Andrew Whitehouse was silent for a few moments. 'Well there's not much use in hiding it, because you'll find out anyway. I didn't. Not really. He was always away working and when he was here, he wasn't exactly a fatherly figure. It's no real secret that we didn't exactly see eye to eye on many things.'

'And what sort of relationship did he have with your mother?'

'She tolerated him. We all tolerated him – some more than others. Neither of us saw much of him. He was always off flouncing about with his floozies and having a good time in his own little showbiz world.'

Hardwick and Flint could sense the anger and resentment boiling up in Andrew Whitehouse, even with very little coercion, and it soon became apparent as to how his temper could quite easily get the better of him.

'Can you describe your movements on Friday night for us? Just so we know we've got everything,' Ellis asked.

'What, all of them? It was a long evening. If you mean did I go into his bedroom, then no. The only upstairs room I went into was my bedroom. Or what's left of it, anyway, after he decided to get rid of all my stuff when I went to university.'

'Mr Whitehouse, did you ever want to kill your father?' Hardwick asked from left field.

'Yes. Many times,' Andrew answered quickly. 'But I didn't do it.'

'I apologise. I have to ask.'

'No, I quite understand.'

'Tell me, how well do you know your parents' gardener, Christos Karagounis?'

'Christos? Not all that well, but then again I've been away at university,' Andrew replied.

'Yes, but before that you were living here with your parents. You must have seen him regularly.'

'Not really. I don't see why I should have had much to do with him. He looked after my parents' garden. That's about it. Although –'

'Yes?' Hardwick asked.

'Well, it was a bit odd, really,' Andrew said, shuffling his weight to his other foot. 'I think Christos had some sort of hold over my parents.'

'A hold?' Hardwick asked, his interest piqued.

'Look, I've no idea what it was, but it's a little bit strange, don't you think? You might like to ask Christos why he was so happy to work for only a few hours a week in my parents' garden, and yet he still managed to live in a terraced house in Shafford, completely rent free.'

'Well, perhaps he was working for other people as well,' Ellis offered.

'He wasn't. He spent all of his spare time at his house. Barely anyone else in the village had ever heard of him, except those who knew him as my parents' gardener. You'd think someone else would have known him if was offering a local service.'

Hardwick said nothing, knowing that this outburst of information would not be the last to leave Andrew Whitehouse's lips.

'I found the mortgage records in my dad's office one day. I knew something was wrong, and to be honest it started to scare me a bit. The house that Christos Karagounis lived in was owned by my dad, and rented by Christos, rent-free. Tell me, why would you buy your gardener a house?'

'Well,' Hardwick said, 'I don't wish to cast aspersions, but your father did have quite a considerable amount of money. Perhaps it was some sort of thank-you for his work.'

'I'm not sure,' Andrew replied. 'If you ask me, Christos Karagounis had some sort of hold over my father. I think he knew more than he should have done.'

As the pair left Westerlea House, Ellis began to tug at Hardwick's sleeve. 'Kempston, why didn't you mention the assault and arrest? We could have put him right on the back foot with that!'

'One thing at a time, Ellis. You really must learn to keep your powder dry. If we go bowling in with everything all at once, we'll have nothing left to use later. Besides, his knowing that we know is going to do us absolutely no favours at all. We're far better off keeping it to ourselves for now. Let him put himself in the hot water; if he's the murderer, he'll need no help from us.'

21

Detective Inspector Rob Warner had never really got used to the sight of dead bodies. He would never let on to any of his colleagues about that, though. Besides, it was the inconvenience that really got up his nose.

He sighed and shook his head as he carefully surveyed the scene around this particular prostrate corpse, the blood pooling and congealing around its head. The forensics team were hard at work taking swabs and picking up hairs, while another white-suited sort took an assortment of photographs and placed down numbered markers. It didn't seem to Warner as though much in the way of scientific input was needed: the large brass candlestick holder, which lay on the floor next to the body, had an impressive amount of blood and brain matter stuck to it.

'Do you reckon they did it with the candlestick holder, guv?' the young DC, Sam Kerrigan, innocently enquired.

'Y'know, I hadn't thought of that, DC Kerrigan,' Warner responded, sarcastically. DC Kerrigan shuffled proudly, his hands shoved in his pockets as the corners of his mouth rose.

'Doesn't look like there was much of a fight,' one of the white-suited forensics sorts said, not taking his eyes from the floor.

'How do you mean?' Warner asked. He never could quite get his head around how the forensics boys managed to work out exactly what had happened just by looking at a pool of blood and a footprint, but then again that was why he was the DI.

'Well, the pattern of the blood spatters on the wall tells us that the blow came from this direction,' the man said, re-enacting the scene almost too realistically, as he raised his arm and brought it down onto the skull of his imaginary victim. 'If you look at how the victim is lying, it seems as though the first blow was probably what did it. There's been no twisting or turning or falling awkwardly. Just a simple crack to the back of the head and—boom—on the deck.'

Warner raised his eyebrows, almost in disbelief at the man's apparent enjoyment of the moment. 'So how do you explain the other spatters on the floor?' he asked, pointing at the array of apparently random splashes on the tiled floor.

'Ah, well quite simply it seems they were done while the victim was already on the floor. It looks as though the victim was struck a number of times after he had fallen.'

'Already dead?' Warner asked.

'Impossible to say. Certainly unconscious, judging by the fact that the fall appears to have broken the victim's nose. Now, I don't know about you, Detective Inspector, but if I fall over I tend to try and land on my hands, not my face. Unless, of course, I'm already unconscious when I hit the ground. Either way, it seems that the killer wanted to make sure the job was done properly. They didn't leave anything to chance.'

'But why do it all with a candlestick holder?' Warner asked. 'Surely, if you wanted someone dead that badly, you'd come equipped. It looks as though the murder weapon came from the mantelpiece,' he said, pointing at the sizeable gap next to the identical model already there; the gap filled only with a shiny round mark where the dust had gathered around the original object.

'I was thinking that myself, guv,' the younger officer said. 'Looks to me as though it could be an argument gone wrong. That would explain the use of an opportunistic weapon rather than something the killer had brought with them.'

'But not the mindless bludgeoning that came after it, DC Kerrigan.'

'How do you mean, guv?'

'Well, let's say I'm standing here in my kitchen and we have an argument. I turn away from you and you bash me over the head with the first thing you find – a candlestick holder. I hit the canvas like a sack of spuds and there's blood pouring from my head. Do you carry on smashing in my skull? No, you're too shocked at what you've done. If this is an argument gone wrong, it would have to go very wrong for you to want to make sure I was completely dead.'

DC Kerrigan said nothing for a few moments, his curled bottom lip betraying the circle of thoughts that were whizzing around his young head.

'It just doesn't add up. If you ask me, it seems to have been a real spur-of-the-moment thing. Whoever killed our victim knew that they had to do it right there and then. No time to get equipped and no chance of a miraculous recovery.'

'Well that makes sense, I guess,' DC Kerrigan said, as he averted his eyes from the victim's open skull. 'So all we need to know is who.'

'Yes, and that's where it gets tricky.'

Over the course of the next fifteen minutes, the pair continued to be shown the intricacies of the crime scene by the forensics team. The lack of forced entry seemed to indicate that the victim had known the killer — they'd been let into the house. They were obviously known well enough to the victim to be invited into the living room. Why, then, would someone so close and familiar see fit to cave in the victim's skull with such sudden ferocity?

'Hardwick, it's DI Warner,' the detective spoke into his mobile phone a few moments later. 'Now, don't go getting too excited—I'm just keeping you in the loop—but we've got another dead body. It's Reverend Michael Winton.'

22

Harry Greenlaw's face conveyed both shock and fear as Hardwick and Flint watched Detective Inspector Rob Warner break the news to him. The faint glow of the street light outside the vicarage was enough to reflect the tears that rolled down the verger's cheek. Out of respect for the moment, Hardwick and Flint kept their distance and stood between Harry Greenlaw and the vicarage, with the intention of speaking to him once Warner had finished the difficult job of explaining what had happened.

'He looks pretty upset, Kempston,' Ellis said.

'Well, wouldn't you be? He's worked for – and practically lived with – the vicar for years. They both dedicated their lives to Tollinghill and now one of their parishioners has taken it upon themselves to repay them with the ultimate insult.'

Ellis picked a leaf off a nearby young birch tree and began to tear the pieces as he spoke. 'Must make it even worse if you're particularly religious, I suppose.'

'How do you mean?' Hardwick asked.

'Well, you and I can put it down to people reacting to situations, or even being naturally evil, but to have to question your own belief in God, and ask what was so bad that he had to allow this to happen... I don't think I could even begin to try and explain that.'

'Fortunately we don't have to, Ellis. That's for Harry Greenlaw and his God to fight out.'

DI Warner brought his difficult conversation to a close with a reassuring hand on Harry Greenlaw's upper back, passing him his police contact card with the other. Harry Greenlaw nodded and DI Warner headed for his car.

'Mr Greenlaw, my condolences,' Hardwick said as the verger walked towards the vicarage.

'Oh, thank you. It's such a shock! I only went out for half an hour and I come back to this. I just don't know what to say,' Harry replied, waving DI Warner's card in the air as he spoke.

'May I ask where you went?' Hardwick asked, as innocently and matter-of-factly as he could.

'Just for a walk. I do it every night. I started when my dog, Bonnie, was alive, but have just carried on since. That's been two years now, but I still enjoy the walk. Tollinghill is so beautiful in the evening, and so–' Harry Greenlaw paused for a moment.

'Safe?' Ellis Flint added.

'Well, yes. It is. That's the horrible thing. That's two murders this week, and I just don't know what to think! Who do you think could be doing this?'

'We don't know, but we intend to find out as quickly as possible,' Hardwick said. 'Mr Greenlaw, I must tell you that Michael Winton came to see me early this afternoon. He said that he was privy to some information from a confession, which may have helped to find Oscar Whitehouse's killer. I don't know what it was, or why he even came to see me, seeing as he couldn't tell me what it was, but I just wondered if you might have any idea what he knew.'

Harry Greenlaw shuffled his feet and thought for a few moments. 'No, none. The priest-penitent bond is sacrosanct, anyway, so he wouldn't have told me either. I thought something was on his mind, though. I knew it!'

'How do you mean?' Ellis asked.

'He had been acting very odd lately. Just little things, you know. Nothing I could put my finger on, but the sort of thing you spot quite easily when you spend so much time with someone. There was this... this look in his eyes. Almost like fear. Like he sensed some sort of danger.'

'Danger?' Ellis Flint asked.

'Yeah, but I can't really explain how. Just... a sort of sixth sense, I guess. It's probably nothing, but you never know what's worth mentioning at a time like this, do you?'

'No, indeed. Well we shan't keep you any longer,' Hardwick said. 'The police will want to speak with you further regarding your whereabouts this evening.'

'Why?' Harry Greenlaw asked, showing a sudden spark of interest. 'I've already told you where I was.'

'Yes, but the police will want to speak to anybody who might be implicated, Mr Greenlaw. When it comes to murder in a small place like Tollinghill, I'm afraid everybody is a suspect.'

23

Hardwick sat nursing his Campari and orange as the jukebox played quietly in the front bar of the Freemason's Arms. He'd not particularly considered this pub to be his local until a case, over eighteen months previous, had very much revolved around it. Having caught the killer, Hardwick always found that he was very welcome at the Freemason's Arms, with more than one or two drinks finding their way to him without any money exchanging hands.

He sat at the bar, as he always did, preferring the proximity of the bar talk and enjoying the wide range of colourful characters that appeared and disappeared every few moments. The ivory crack of a striking cue ball reverberated from the pool table as he tried to imagine the vicar's last moments at the mercy of his own candlestick holder. The incongruity between the spontaneity and ferocity of the attack was playing on his mind as his sipped his drink, the ice cube caressing his upper lip.

The door to the lounge bar creaked as it opened, revealing the familiar stature of Dolores Mickelwhite. She almost jogged over to the bar with an eagerness Hardwick had rarely seen in someone of her age.

'Can I buy you a drink?' Hardwick asked, as the woman beckoned him over to a table.

'Oh, no, thank you. I shan't stay long. I just wanted to speak to you about what happened last night at the Old Vicarage.'

'I'm afraid there's not much I can tell you, Ms Mickelwhite,' Hardwick explained, pulling out a chair and preparing to dodge the barrage of invasive questions, which were sure to come his way. 'Besides, certain types of... talk... can be detrimental to an investigation.'

'Oh, no. Not this type of talk, Mr Hardwick,' she replied, I think you'll find this very interesting indeed.

'Modus vivendi, Ms Mickelwhite,' Hardwick said, raising his glass.

'Oh? Had they run out of Campari, then?' she said, determined to continue. 'You see, the thing is this. I was out for a short evening walk last night, and at the time that the vicar was killed, I was walking past the Old Vicarage.'

'Did you tell the police this?' Hardwick asked, his interest suddenly aroused.

'Oh, no. They haven't asked me anything,' she replied. Hardwick felt quite sure that Dolores Mickel-white didn't usually need to be asked to provide informa-tion. 'Anyway, I was walking past the eastern wall of the grounds—it's just below my head height—and I happened to peer over and see somebody walking quite purposefully up to the front door.'

'Did you see who it was? Surely it was too dark by then.'

'Oh, it was pitch black. But the curtains in the front windows hadn't been drawn and there was a lot of light coming from them. I could see exactly who it was, Mr Hardwick, as clearly as if it had been the middle of the day.'

'Who, Ms Mickelwhite?' Hardwick implored, his patience being tested.

'It was Oscar Whitehouse.'

24

'With the greatest of respect, Ms Mickelwhite, Oscar Whitehouse has been dead since Friday night,' Hardwick said, discounting her testimony and wondering how quickly he could get back to the bar for another Campari and orange.

'I know!' Dolores shrieked with excitement. 'That's why I came to see you! The police would never believe me if I told them, but I know you to be a man of rational thought, Mr Hardwick. We all know your reputation for solving mysteries!'

'Even my talents stop short of raising the dead, Ms Mickelwhite,' Hardwick replied. 'I'm afraid it's simply not possible.'

'That's where you're wrong, Mr Hardwick,' Dolores

said, rummaging in her handbag and retrieving a VHS cassette. 'And this will show you why!'

Moments later, Hardwick, Dolores, and the recently arrived Ellis Flint were sitting in Dolores Mickelwhite's living room as she fumbled to cram the VHS cassette into her video recorder, having quite literally dragged Hardwick up the road from the Freemason's Arms to her cottage.

'Darned new technology. Can never get these things in properly,' she muttered as way of apology.

'With all due respect, Ms Mickelwhite, DVDs and network storage don't have that problem,' Ellis Flint piped up.

'All Greek to me, love. These damned things are difficult enough without me fiddling about with inter-nets and digi-dicks. Ah, there we go.' Dolores Mickel-white retreated from the television set and perched on the edge of her armchair, her fingers prodding at the remote control like a vet giving CPR to a hamster. 'I'm never around to see it myself, but I always make sure I record it.'

'Record what, Ms Mickelwhite?' Hardwick asked.

'The Afternoon Show, of course. I never miss it.

That Darwin O'Hare makes me laugh, he really does. Wonderful sense of humour.'

'Uh... we're not here to watch daytime television, are we, Ms Mickelwhite?' Hardwick said as he prepared to rise from his chair and make a quick exit.

'Of a sort. But bear with me, please. How the hell does this thing fast-for... Ah! There we go. It's just after the bit where he... Yep, here we go.'

The picture stayed frozen for a moment, and then the tape began to play.

'—almost solely on your belief that our spirits live on after death. Do you expect that this book will convince the nay-sayers that the paranormal world is real?'

'No, I expect there will always be cynics. However, I know that the world will soon have proof of life after death. That much is true. Evil will always live on.'

Dolores Mickelwhite paused the tape and glanced expectantly at Hardwick and Flint. Hardwick raised one eyebrow, whilst Flint sat nonplussed. Dolores Mickelwhite pressed a button on the remote control and the tape rewound a few seconds and played again.

. . .

'I know that the world will soon have proof of life after death. That much is true. Evil will always live on.'

'Ms Mickelwhite, that's all very interesting, but what exactly are you trying to say?'

'Can't you see, Kempston?' Ellis Flint interjected, his excitement growing by the second. 'He said it himself! "The world will soon have proof of life after death." He said those words on live TV just hours before he died! He said he would prove that evil will always live on!'

'Ellis, are you seriously trying to tell me that you think Oscar Whitehouse came back from the dead to kill the vicar?'

Without waiting for an answer, Hardwick sighed heavily and left the house.

'It's perfectly plausible, Kempston!' Flint shouted as he chased the fast-walking Hardwick down the gravel path.

'People do not just come back from the dead, Ellis. There's a perfectly reasonable explanation, I'm sure. And one that doesn't involve ghosts and ghoulies.'

'It's not ghosts and ghoulies, Kempston – it's the spirit world, the astral plane! If Oscar Whitehouse had only just died it's perfectly possible that his energy would still be vibrant!'

'It is not perfectly possible, Ellis. It is absolute tosh. There was no energy – vibrant or otherwise – except the force that brought the candlestick holder down on the vicar's head.'

'Yes! The force of Oscar Whitehouse's spirit!'

'Oh, for... Ghosts do not exist, Ellis! And even if they did, they certainly wouldn't walk around villages smashing people's skulls in with candlestick holders.'

'But why not? Think about it – if ghosts can close doors and switch on lights, why not smack someone round the head?'

'Ghosts cannot close doors and switch on lights, Ellis! Draughts close doors and electrical faults switch on lights. Short of a bloody hurricane-force draught, neither of those phenomena are capable of caving in someone's skull. Now, will you please leave this supernatural nonsense alone?'

'All right. What's your explanation then?' Flint asked, seeming very cock-sure of himself.

'I'm not entirely sure. What I am sure of, though, is that there is a perfectly rational one.'

25

The young lady at the front desk smiled as she handed
Hardwick the pass card which would allow him to enter
the records office. Although most such institutions had
long since been amalgamated into libraries, the records
office at Bradstow (the town, forty-five miles from
Tollinghill, where Oscar Whitehouse was born)
remained stoically independent, fending off the advent
of technological advancement, much the same as the rest
of the village.

The sheer volume of cabinets and screens over-
whelmed him. He was amazed at the number of records
available for the relatively small area of Bradstow. The
generations of history stood before him, as blatant as
they could ever be, as Hardwick scanned the indices for
the location of the files he sought.

Having written down Oscar Whitehouse's name and date of birth, Hardwick handed it to the registrar, helped himself to a 'coffee' from the adjacent machine, and sat down on the ripped leather chair. Eyeing the selection of leaflets and guides available on the low table next to him, he took a sip of the bitter liquid; his face contorted in disgust. He picked up a dog-eared copy of Country Living and thumbed through the well-worn pages. An article on a Dorset farm, which still practised the traditional method of sheep shearing, was followed by a fascinating piece on the best fertilisers to use for growing scallions. Hardwick's patience was saved by the reappearance of the registrar, her spectacles delicately balanced on the bridge of her nose as she ruffled the printed copy of Oscar Whitehouse's birth certificate.

'It's all here,' the registrar stated. 'I hope this is the one you're looking for.'

Hardwick mentally noted the information on the birth certificate.

WHITEHOUSE

When and where born: Twentieth May 1957, 3h 30m p.m. Bradstow.

Forename(s), if any: Oscar Bertrand Kingsley

Sex: Boy

Name and surname of father: Bertrand Whitehouse
Name, surname and maiden name of mother: Annie Elizabeth Whitehouse, formerly Kingsley
Occupation of father: Agricultural labourer

'Thank you,' Hardwick said, still perusing the document. 'Tell me, are there any other birth certificates issued to the same parents on the same day?'

'No,' the registrar replied instantly. 'If there were, I'd have found it in the same section as this one.'

'So Oscar Whitehouse was the only child born to these parents on this day?'

The registrar disappeared for another moment to double-check her computer records.

'Absolutely,' she said on her return.

'Were any other children born to the same parents? Or, with the same surname and around the same time?'

'Extra certificates will incur an additional fee, sir,' the registrar said.

'That's fine.'

The registrar delivered another few cursory taps to the computer keyboard. 'Nope. Nothing. No babies with the surname Whitehouse were born within nine years in this district, and even afterwards any babies with the same surname were born to completely different parents.'

'Can you take a closer look at the parents? Did they have any other children?'

A few more taps were delivered to the keyboard.

'None at all. His parents, Annie and Bertrand — neither had any other children, together or apart.'

'So Oscar Whitehouse was, without doubt, an only child?'

The registrar sighed and looked down her glasses at Hardwick as she began to lose her patience. 'Yes, sir. Without any shadow of a doubt.'

'And tell me, when and how did Oscar Whitehouse's parents die?'

Turning back to her computer to bring up the death certificates for both Annie and Bertrand Whitehouse, the registrar raised an eyebrow as she read the details on both documents.

'They have the same date of death. They both died in a car accident, it seems.'

Hardwick thanked the registrar as he scribbled the last of his notes in his leather-bound notebook and paid his now-extortionate bill.

Hardwick mulled the case over in his mind later that day

as he sauntered back up Tollinghill High Street from the train station, mentally running through the different possibilities of the events which led to the murder of Oscar Whitehouse. He was roused from his daydream by the voice of Harry Greenlaw, who was shouting at him from across to the street.

Turning to look, Hardwick watched the verger jog across the road, laden with shopping bags in both hands, as he caught him up.

'Stroke of luck finding you here. How's the investigation going?'

'Slowly, but we'll get there,' Hardwick said, as the pair continued to walk.

'I hope so. I've just been in the shop, there, getting some groceries together. The oddest thing – then again, nothing is ever unusual for Tollinghill – but, I overheard Dolores Mickelwhite talking to a few of the locals.'

'Oh yes?' Hardwick asked, his interest suddenly aroused.

'Yeah, something about having seen Oscar Whitehouse in the churchyard a few days after he died. She seems to think his ghost came back to kill the reverend!'

'Honestly, that woman –'

'I mean,' the verger interrupted. 'I'm a spiritual man, as you know, but coming back from the dead? To commit murder? That's all a little far-fetched, don't you think?'

'Indeed it is. I would take no notice of her, if I were you. The woman's more than a little mad.'

'Oh yes, everybody around here knows that. She comes out with some outrageous gossip at times. I think she's actually quite lonely. If you ask me, that kind of scurrilous tittle-tattle will only ever land you in a lot of trouble. But anyway, I thought you might like to know, seeing as it's connected with your investigation and all.'

'Thank you, Mr Greenlaw. Much appreciated.'

26

Hardwick sat in his armchair, one finger curled in front of his lips, his foot tapping rhythmically on the hardwood floor as Ellis Flint slowly lost his patience.

'Kempston, you're doing it again,' Ellis Flint remarked.

'Mmmmm?' came the response as Hardwick's brow furrowed further and the tapping increased both in frequency and volume.

'Kempston!' yelled Flint, as he jumped up from his own chair and slammed his hand down onto Hardwick's thigh. 'Will you stop it!'

'For Christ's... You only need to ask!' Hardwick snapped out of his trance and rubbed his sore leg.

'I did. Five times! You're doing that thing where you zone out and completely ignore what's going on around you. Usually means there's something on your mind. Care to share?'

'There's nothing to share, Ellis.'

'There must be something. Something's on your mind, clearly.'

'Well, yes. Something is on my mind – nothing.'

'I haven't got time for riddles, Kempston. Just tell me.'

'No, you don't understand. That's the problem, Ellis. The problem is that there's nothing. I went to the General Records Office in Bradstow this morning. I thought that one explanation for Dolores Mickelwhite seeing Oscar Whitehouse days after he died was that perhaps he had a twin.'

'And he didn't?' Ellis asked hopefully.

'No. Not a single sibling of any sort, twin or otherwise.'

'So does that mean you're starting to believe that it really was the ghost of Oscar Whitehouse that she saw?' Ellis asked after a few moments' considered silence.

'No, Ellis. That's simply not an option.'

'But why not? I've been doing quite a lot of research, actually. I think you'd be surprised how often things like this happen.'

'Oh dear...' Hardwick sighed, resigned to his fate.

'No, seriously. I've spent this morning reading up

on things and it's absolutely incredible, some of the
stuff that goes on; disappearances, spiritual images,
premonitions, all sorts of things. It's actually really
interesting once you open your mind and start to look
into it. Have you ever heard of the Greenbrier Ghost,
Kempston?'

'No, Ellis, I haven't...' Hardwick exhaled, with his
forehead resting on his palm.

'I was reading about it earlier today,' Ellis replied,
thumbing through a selection of printed papers to find
the details. 'Here we are. In 1897, a young woman called
Elva Zona Heaster was murdered in West Virginia in
the United States. After her death, she appeared in her
mother's dreams to tell her about the man who killed
her. Her ghost said that her killer had broken her neck.
When the police exhumed her body, they found her
neck had been broken and that she had been choked –
just like Oscar Whitehouse!'

'Oscar Whitehouse's neck wasn't broken, Ellis.'

'No, but he was choked! Don't you see the
connection?'

'Ellis, thousands of people are choked to death every
year. One incident from 1897 is hardly–'

'That's not all, Kempston. The dream actually led
the police to catch her killer and the testimony of Elva's
ghost was used at the murderer's trial.'

'Well, the Americans are very strange people, Ellis. Nothing ever surprises me about them.'

'Open your mind, Kempston! What about Hammersmith?'

'What about it?'

'Are the people from there strange as well?' Ellis asked, retrieving another sheet of paper from his stack.

'No stranger than most Londoners.'

'Good. Because there's another incident known as the Hammersmith Ghost murder case. In 1803, a number of people in the Hammersmith area had reported being attacked by a ghost. One woman was attacked just before Christmas in a graveyard near her house. She survived the ordeal for long enough to describe a white spectre that had risen from a grave and strangled her until she fainted. She then died a few days later.'

'Ellis, people are incredibly strange. Rather than accepting that nothing happened at all, they will come up with the most remarkable deductions involving ghosts, aliens and spirits in order to try and explain what is actually incredibly mundane.'

'So what you're trying to say is that Dolores Mickelwhite didn't see anything at all? That she just imagined the whole thing? That she's mad? Lying? Blind?'

'Who knows? She may well have thought she saw

something. How often do we swear blind that we caught some sort of movement out of the corner of our eye? Or have that feeling that we're being watched? We all experience these things, but most are sensible enough to put them down to tricks of the mind. The mind is a remarkable thing, Ellis. I've also done a lot of reading on the subject in my time, although I must add, my research has been somewhat less biased. The human brain is a huge network of minute and precise electrical signals. When precision fails in the brain, odd things can seem to happen. But that's exactly where it stays — in the mind. We need to be careful not to confuse our mind's thoughts with outside factors. Not everything is down to external stimuli. Some people, on the other hand, will deliberately invent things for attention.'

'Do you think she's one of those?'

'It's entirely possible. What do you know about Dolores Mickelwhite, Ellis?'

Ellis thought for a moment. 'Not a whole lot, if I'm honest. I mean, I see her in the village most days and we talk a lot, but I don't really know anything about her. Most of the time she's asking questions or talking about local gossip. She always seems to know everything about everyone else, but never reveals a thing about herself, now I come to think about it.'

'The dark horse, some might say?'

'I guess so. Probably more of an attention seeker if you ask me. But do you think that makes her a killer?'

'It's a possibility, Ellis. Everybody's a suspect. Unfortunately some make themselves far more suspicious than others. I think it's time we paid Ms Mickelwhite another visit, don't you?'

27

The wisteria tickled Hardwick's hair as he rang Dolores Mickelwhite's doorbell. Brushing the errant plant away, he waited for a few moments before he resorted to using the heavy knocker, which adorned the front of the large wooden door. The face of the iron gremlin stared back at him, as he removed his hand from it.

'It's a pagan thing,' Ellis said, to be met with an inquisitive look from Hardwick. 'The gremlin-style door knocker. It's meant to protect the house from evil spirits.'

'Yes, well it's remarkably ugly, whatever its purpose.'

Another few moments passed. Kneeling, Hardwick peered through the letterbox into the hallway of the cottage. Towards the back of the hall he could just about make out the doorway into the kitchen, its brown wooden cupboard doors and white tiled floor. A coat appeared to be hanging on the wall in the hallway and the light of the telephone answering machine blinked in the darkened room.

'Hello? Ms Mickelwhite? It's Kempston Hardwick and Ellis Flint. Can we have a word?'

The letterbox snapped shut and Hardwick rose to his feet.

'Maybe she's out,' Ellis said.

'Do you leave the living room lights and television on when you go out, Ellis?' Hardwick asked, gesturing to the living room window.

'Sometimes, if I forget.'

'Does Dolores Mickelwhite strike you as the sort of woman who forgets? Oh no, she's far sharper than any of us, Ellis. That's the worrying thing. You stay here; I'm going to take a look round the back.'

The open-plan exterior of the cottage made it easy for Hardwick to make his way round to the back of the building, sat, as it was, in the middle of its own continuous garden. The thatch looked recent and the walls seemed to be free of rising damp or any sort of defects. This was clearly a very well-looked-after cottage. It struck Hardwick as perhaps a little too well looked after, for a high-maintenance cottage lived in by a single woman of advancing years.

As he walked around the right-hand side of the

cottage and reached the back of the building, the first and second windows showed him a view of the traditional kitchen. The aga looked to have been recently used and the sink, full of washing-up, contained fresh bubbles. Moving along the back of the cottage, the next window showed a remarkably neat utility room and bathroom. He barely had time to register the contents of the room when his attention was stolen by the sound of Ellis Flint shouting his name from the front of the cottage.

Rushing towards the sound of Ellis's voice, Hardwick found him peering in through the living-room window to the left-hand side of the front door. Previously obscured by the wisteria, Ellis had battled his way through the triffids to take a look through the window. As Hardwick now did the same, he saw the white-stockinged feet protruding from behind the sofa.

'Help me get this door open, Ellis,' Hardwick barked.

'With what?'

'Use your head, man!'

Flint paused for a few moments, mulling this over.

'I didn't mean... Oh, for... Just get it open, Ellis!'

Shaping up to deliver his killer blow, Flint jiggled his shoulders and ran at the door, lifting his right boot at the vital moment to send a sharp shock – not through the solid wooden door, but through his own leg.

As Flint winced in pain and hobbled about on the cobbles, Hardwick depressed the iron thumb-latch and the door opened with a click.

'What?' Ellis cried with incredulity. 'Why the hell did you tell me to kick it in if it was open the whole time?'

'I didn't tell you to kick it in, Ellis. I told you to get it open. Why must you always insist on doing things the hard way?'

Darting into the living room, Hardwick rounded the door and was met by the full, unobstructed view of the dead body of Dolores Mickelwhite.

28

'Well that's that theory blown out of the water, then,' Ellis remarked as the medical staff removed Dolores Mickelwhite's lifeless body.

'Which theory?' Hardwick asked, his eyes glued to the events going on around him.

'Your theory about her being the killer.'

'I had no theory, Ellis. Only aspects for elimination. And yes, that one now seems to be a little less likely.'

'A little?' Ellis asked, seemingly offended at Hardwick's remarks.

'Her being dead doesn't automatically mean she didn't kill Oscar Whitehouse or the vicar, Ellis. You don't receive immunity from suspicion just because you've subsequently died.'

The familiar figure of Detective Inspector Rob

Warner approached the pair and removed his notebook and pen from his inside jacket pocket.

'So run me through what happened, exactly. You two just happened to turn up here and find Dolores Mickelwhite dead?'

'Essentially, yes,' Hardwick said, matter-of-factly. 'We came to speak to her about what she thought she saw on the night that the vicar died.'

'Which was?'

Hardwick sighed. 'She thought she saw Oscar Whitehouse entering the churchyard and heading for the vicarage.'

'Oscar Whitehouse?' the detective asked. 'But he'd been dead for days at that point.'

'Yes, exactly. So she was clearly either imagining things, or had been making it up all along. Personally, the possibility of the latter struck me as more than a little suspicious.'

'Well yes, it is. So you thought you'd not bother to tell the police. Instead, you came round here on your own and trampled all over a crime scene?'

'We didn't know it was a crime scene at the time, DI Warner. It was only when we got here that we found Ms Mickelwhite dead. Fortunately, it seems it had only happened shortly before we arrived, so you should probably thank us for preserving the fresh evidence. Had we not turned up, I doubt if many people would have rushed round to check on her over the next few days.'

'Thank you?' DI Warner asked, with a touch of shock at Hardwick's temerity. 'Listen, Hardwick. We asked for your input on how Oscar Whitehouse could have died, but to be honest, now I'm starting to regret it. You've no right to continue stepping on our toes. We've now got three bodies on our hands and people are going to start asking questions. Do you see what I mean?'

'Perfectly, DI Warner.'

'Because, as I see it, the closer you get to a potential suspect or witness, the next thing we know is they've wound up dead. In fact, I'm feeling a little nervous just standing here talking to you now, and will probably sleep with a baseball bat under my pillow tonight.'

'All I want is to see the killer caught, Detective Inspector.'

'You and me both, Hardwick. You and me both. But at the moment, your gallivanting seems to be causing more trouble than it's worth. We've clearly got a killer who will stop at nothing to make sure that we never discover the truth about what happened to Oscar White-house. The closer you get, the more people die. Will you at least try and keep some semblance of distance?'

Hardwick simply smiled, and left.

29

The noise in the Freemason's Arms that evening grew steadily louder as the number of patrons increased. Hardwick and Flint sat in the far corner, away from the bar, in the regency-style armchairs. If there was one thing that could tempt Hardwick away from the hustle and bustle of the bar, it was a regency-style armchair.

'They've all got to be connected somehow, Kempston. I mean, think about it. Oscar Whitehouse dies and the vicar tells us he knows a big secret, which he can't divulge. Next thing we know, he's dead. Lo and behold, Dolores Mickelwhite swears blind she saw the dead Oscar Whitehouse present at the time the vicar was killed. Not only is that physically impossible, but Dolores Mickelwhite herself is killed shortly after. I don't know about you, Kempston, but it looks as though someone is desperate to cover something up here.'

'Indeed. And I think we need to tread carefully ourselves, Ellis. DI Warner is right.'

'Christ. I never thought I'd hear you say those words, Kempston. But if we back off, surely the killer's free and loose.'

'You mentioned the pattern yourself. Every time someone has some information that might lead to the killer, they end up being the next victim. I don't know about you, Ellis, but I plan on putting up with many more years in this mortal coil.'

'What? Do you think you might be next?'

'Well, I'm certainly the closest person to catching the killer. Judging by his or her past form, I would say I'm probably next in line.'

'Jesus. So what are you going to do?' Ellis asked.

'I'm going to smoke our killer out, Ellis. It seems that the talk of the village has once again been Tollinghill's downfall. The reverend intimated rather too loudly that he had information which could lead to the killer's identity, and he wound up dead. Dolores Mickelwhite stormed around the village telling all and sundry that she had seen – well – something, at the scene of the vicar's murder. Hours later, she's dead too. I'm going to put the word about that I'll be at Westerlea House later tonight. Eliza and Andrew Whitehouse are in London until eight o'clock, so I'll ask everyone to convene at eight-thirty for my arrival at nine. I think we can quite safely assume that our killer will probably be lying in wait for me.'

'But surely that's dangerous!' Ellis exclaimed, almost jumping up from his seat.

'Ellis, if one never faces danger then one can never succeed. You cannot shoot your enemy without putting your head above the parapet.'

'No, but that's completely different to inviting a murderer to try and kill you!'

'Is it? Is it really? No, I think it's actually a very good plan. Whoever our killer is, they only strike when someone declares that they know something. So, I'm going to declare that I know something. That way, the killer will put their very own head above the parapet, and I'll be ready and waiting.'

'It sounds like a stupid idea to me!' Ellis replied, trying to keep his voice stern yet as low as possible in order to avoid anyone overhearing their conversation. 'What if the murderer ends up killing you too?'

'They won't. The previous victims had no idea they were about to become victims. All they knew is that they had some clues that might lead to the killer's identity. They weren't ready and prepared for what was coming. I, on the other hand, will be.'

30

'Nice of Eliza Whitehouse to leave you a key, Kempston,' Ellis Flint said as they unlocked the front door to Westerlea House at seven o'clock that evening.

'She left everyone a key, Ellis, without even knowing it. If it wasn't under the doormat, it had to be under the plant pot. Some people seem to enjoy both being a target for burglars and voiding their home insurance in one stupid move.'

The door creaked open and the pair entered. Hardwick purposefully led the way up the grand staircase to the upper landing. The walk seemed longer than usual, with each step feeling like a huge leap into the unknown.

'Oscar Whitehouse's bedroom, Ellis. The room in which he was murdered.'

'I know. We've gone over the room with a fine-tooth comb. What's this all about?'

'The locked room! One of the staples of a murder mystery, Ellis.'

'What, so you're saying you know how the killer got into a room, committed a murder and got back out again, despite the room being locked from the inside?'

'That little conundrum was never one which baffled me, no. The real question was who and why.'

'Well, at the moment my question is how?'

'Oh, quite easily, Ellis. The door wasn't locked from the inside at all.'

'Yes it was – the key was in the inside. It landed on the floor when the door was barged open.'

'Did anyone ever see the key on the inside of the door?'

'Yes. Major Fulcrupp said Dolores Mickelwhite looked through the keyhole and couldn't see anything because the key was in there.'

'Let's take that one step at a time, Ellis. Dolores Mickelwhite looked through the keyhole and couldn't see anything. Correct. Because the key was in there? Not necessarily so. Something was in the lock, I grant you. And one might rightly expect it to be a key, but if you look closely,' Hardwick said, bending down, 'you'll see that it's actually filled with glue.'

'But the key fell out of the lock and onto the floor!'

'No, they heard it fall out of the lock and onto the floor. Or, rather, they thought they heard it.' Hardwick walked over to the dresser on the right-hand side of the room. 'When I inspected the room, I found this,' he said, picking up the brass clothes hook, which lay in the crumpled dressing gown. 'At first glance, it seems to fit perfectly on the wall here, next to the en-suite bathroom. The screw holes match up perfectly.'

'So what's that got to do with anything?'

'Look at the back, Ellis. The hook has sticky pads on the back of it. The papered wall, however, shows no sign of having had an adhesive stuck to it. The wallpaper is spotless. I didn't notice that small detail at the time and stuck it onto the wall — back onto it, as far as I was concerned. As you can see, it's already fallen off. Damned infernal sticky pads. You see, this brass hook used to be attached to the wall here — with screws — but has since been moved to the main door. Not wanting to screw holes in such a beautiful wooden door, the Whitehouses instead used the sticky pads to adhere the hook to the back of the door.'

'So?' Ellis asked.

'So, we all know how terrible these little sticky pads are. When I found the brass hook and dressing gown in a heap just below the place where the dressing gown used to hang, it was complete coincidence. The dressing gown had been left there carelessly – probably because the hook that had been stuck to the back of the door with these infernal sticky pads, was now so unreliable. When the door was barged open on Friday evening, it wasn't the key which hit the floor at all; it was this brass hook.'

'So it came off the back of the door, hit the floor and skidded into the heaped dressing gown?'

'Precisely, Ellis.'

'But that doesn't change the fact that the door was locked from the inside! The key was found inside the room!'

'You're being short-sighted again, Ellis. It's one of the oldest tricks in the book. The door is, in fact, locked from the outside. Our killer then placed the key on a sheet of newspaper, and pushed it under the door, leaving just enough to hold on to. A quick shake of the newspaper before pulling it back out ensures that the key is on the floor on the inside of the room. Not foolproof, but the sound of the brass hook hitting the floor was certainly a big turn-up for the books in the killer's eyes.'

'That's remarkable. So the killer entered and left through the bedroom door after all?'

'Indeed. The obvious solution is often the correct one. It's the human brain that raises these imaginary obstacles and makes it seem as though it's not possible.'

'That doesn't tell us anything about who the killer is, though, Kempston.'

'On the contrary, Ellis. We're closer now to our killer than we ever have been.' Hardwick turned around and left Oscar Whitehouse's bedroom. He then knocked on the door of one of the locked spare bedrooms. 'It's over. You may as well come out now.'

31

By eight-thirty the living room at Westerlea House was again as full as it had been on the previous Friday night. The widowed Eliza Whitehouse, her son Andrew, Harry Greenlaw, Major Fulcrupp, Christos Karagounis and Sandy Baker sat in silence as Hardwick and Flint entered the room.

'Ladies and gentlemen. It would be fair to say that up until an hour or so ago, I did not know for certain the identity of the murderer — or murderers — of Oscar Whitehouse, Reverend Michael Winton or Dolores Mickelwhite. I had my suspicions, but they were suspicions that needed additional confirmation, as I shall explain.'

'Is there really any need for all this showmanship?' Andrew Whitehouse asked. 'We're not in some second-rate mystery novel! And where are the police? Shouldn't they be here?'

'Believe me, this is by far the easiest way to explain to everyone what has happened and who the killer is. And don't worry — the police aren't far away at all.'

The silence in the room grew even more poignant as Hardwick continued to explain.

'During the course of this investigation I visited the General Records Office in Bradstow. When a supposedly dead person is spotted at the scene of a later crime, one certainly has to begin to think outside the box. Although the explanation might seem impossible, there were only ever really a small handful of explanations. One possibility was that Oscar Whitehouse may have had a doppelgänger or sibling, who could easily be mistaken for him. That would explain how he came to be seen at the vicarage days after he had died. My visit to the Records Office showed no evidence of a birth certificate for any sibling whatsoever, which means that that particular theory fell very much on its face,' Hardwick explained.

'That was until this afternoon, when I suddenly recalled a particular piece of information from Oscar Whitehouse's own birth certificate. His date and place of birth read: "Twentieth May 1957, 3h 30m p.m. Bradstow."'

'Excuse me for asking,' Major Fulcrupp interrupted, 'but what does his date and place of birth more than fifty-five years ago have to do with who killed him?'

'Quite a lot, actually,' Hardwick continued. 'Not only does it state the date and place of his birth, but it also states the time. An innocent detail quite easily overlooked, I grant you, but what if I were to tell you that birth certificates in England and Wales only ever state the specific time of birth if more than one child was born to the same parents on the same day?'

'What, you mean twins?' Sandy Baker asked.

'Indeed, or triplets, quadruplets, or any other type of multiple birth. That then confirmed to me that Oscar Whitehouse was not an only child at all. However, in the absence of a birth certificate for the sibling, there was very little I could do. Even if a twin had been adopted or somehow moved elsewhere, there'd be a paper trail. So we were left with two possibilities: either the presence of the time on the birth certificate was an error and Oscar Whitehouse was indeed an only child, or somewhere out there there's a twin without any sort of paper trail. That was something I couldn't explain. Until tonight, that is.'

Hardwick walked the few short paces to the living room door and turned the knob, the click of the latch reverberating around the stunned room. The lone figure stood solemnly in the doorway, whilst Detective

Inspector Rob Warner and Detective Constable Sam Kerrigan loomed behind, each holding on to an arm of the killer.

'This, ladies and gentlemen, is the man whom Dolores Mickelwhite saw at the scene of the vicar's murder. The man who introduced himself to me earlier this evening as Malcolm Whitehouse, Oscar's twin.'

A fusion of gasps and shaking heads played out around the living room as Malcolm's eyes bore into those of Kempston Hardwick, neither man breaking the stare.

'Of course, it would be remarkably easy for someone who looks identical to Oscar Whitehouse to wander around the upstairs landing of Westerlea House and go in and out of the master bedroom, arousing absolutely no suspicion whatsoever. He could walk around with ease, committing the crime in his own time without any worry about being seen. As far as anybody else knew, they were looking at Oscar Whitehouse.'

Major Fulcrupp was incredulous. 'But we saw Oscar that evening! He came downstairs! We even spoke to him, for Christ's sake!'

'No, you saw someone come downstairs. Even from a distance, his brother looked slightly different, but then again, that was to be expected with a virus or a fever. A little bit of talcum powder to lighten the complexion, eh, Mrs Whitehouse? One might say he looked rather... ill.'

'It was twins all along! I knew it! And it was Malcolm Whitehouse I saw on the landing that night; not Oscar!' Major Fulcrupp exclaimed, somehow seeing fit to take the credit for the solution to the case.

'Not quite, Major,' Hardwick said, still not diverting his eyes from those of the killer. 'Yet again, we all allowed our minds to run away with themselves, taking as fact things which had never actually been confirmed to be so. We were looking for Oscar Whitehouse's killer when, all along, we should have been looking for Malcolm Whitehouse's killer. Isn't that right, Oscar?'

The room fell into stunned silence, save for the sound of Eliza Whitehouse sobbing in the corner. It was only then that the killer's eyes lost their contact with Hardwick's, his face softening and his head bowed towards his chest as he began to speak.

'It's true. I'm Oscar,' the man said, his voice straining not to break as he spoke. The room remained silent for a few moments as those who attended waited for him to continue and explain. 'Eliza and I met in the mid-seventies. We were both eighteen.' He raised his head to meet the eyes of the sobbing Eliza White-house, a solitary tear running down his cheek as he did so. 'She was my world. So when I found out that she had been sleeping with my brother–' The killer snapped his head away from Eliza's stare and burrowed his chin back into his chest, his face a picture of pain and angst.

'I never meant to–' Eliza attempted to speak through sobs and tears.

'I couldn't bear it,' the killer interrupted loudly, raising his head once more. 'I couldn't possibly stay. I had a complete and utter breakdown. My head was in all sorts of places and I just didn't know what to do. All I knew is that I had to get out of Bradstow as quickly as I possibly could. I didn't even bother to pack a bag. I just went with the clothes on my back. I hitch-hiked down to Portsmouth and stowed away on the ferry to Cherbourg — the Viking Victory. I'll never forget that name as long as I live. For a few fleeting moments I felt like a Viking myself; going to explore the New World in my own illegal way. I never had a passport. I managed to travel the six-hundred or so miles all the way to Aubagne, through a combination of walking, hitch-hiking and trains paid for by working menial jobs. It took me about a week and a half.'

'Aubagne?' Major Fulcrupp asked, recognising the significance of the place. 'You mean to say you joined the French Foreign Legion?'

'Yes. I spent five years in the Légion étrangère, after which they provide you with a new identity and passport. In those days, they could also destroy your old identity and would deny your existence, if you requested it. It used to happen more than you'd think. It wasn't exactly what I expected it all to be, but then again all I wanted was a new start. I didn't want to be Oscar Whitehouse any more. That life and that name had been sullied. I just wanted to start again. I didn't see much action, other than at Kolwezi, in Zaïre, but that only lasted a matter of hours.'

'Absolutely ridiculous battle, that,' Major Fulcrupp saw fit to add.

'I spent the rest of my time in the colonies and on peacekeeping missions in Chad. A bit of time in Algeria and Côte d'Ivoire, otherwise it was just a case of ticking off the days until I could leave and begin my new life under my new identity. I was told my new name the moment I arrived at the Legion. After five years of perfect service I was given full French citizenship.'

'We thought you were dead!' Eliza Whitehouse exclaimed.

'To all intents and purposes, I was. I killed off my old life there and then. It was you who kept Oscar White-house alive, Eliza, not me.'

'So what,' Sandy said. 'You just decided that Malcolm would suddenly take on Oscar's identity? How on Earth could that possibly ever work?'

'It seemed like the easiest thing to do at the time.

Malcolm had a juvenile criminal record. Just a stupid thing, really... a boys' prank gone wrong.'

'What sort of boys' prank, Mrs Whitehouse?' Hardwick asked.

'I don't know the details. He was out with a couple of friends one afternoon and they were playing with some matches in the stairwell of a block of flats. Next thing they knew, the whole complex was ablaze. It sounds daft, but it was on his record.

'By the time Oscar disappeared, the boys had no family left – their parents died a couple of years before and the boys had lived alone since the age of seventeen. They were practically identical in every way, so it wouldn't have been difficult to say that Malcolm was Oscar and that Malcolm had gone to live elsewhere. Not that the boys really spoke to many people locally, anyway. They were both loners from a young age. In the end, we decided that all we really needed to do was leave Bradstow and start again. We never kept in touch with anyone from there after we moved to Tollinghill. After thirty-something years, I suppose people forgot we ever existed.'

'But what about the birth certificates? Why was there only one?' Sandy asked.

'Because Eliza and Malcolm weren't the only ones who had the idea of an identity swap,' the real Oscar

Whitehouse said. 'In five years with the Legion, I built up an exemplary record and ensured I became one of their best recruits. When I requested that all traces of my old identity be destroyed, they did just that. That had been my plan all along. That was why I told the Legion my former identity was Malcolm Whitehouse. I wanted to see him erased from the face of the Earth for what he did to me, and, on paper, he was. To this day I don't know how, but they even managed to ensure that Malcolm Whitehouse had never officially existed in the UK.'

'Which made it a whole lot easier for the real Malcolm to live under the assumed identity of Oscar in the UK, quite confident in the fact that his real identity could never be discovered,' Hardwick said, with his eyes firmly on the killer. 'But it wasn't the romantic happily-ever-after ending you hoped it would be, was it, Eliza?'

The momentary silence was broken by Eliza White-house, avoiding the question, resigned to her fate. 'When the real Oscar came back to England and found me, I immediately fell in love with him all over again. Who wouldn't, when you'd lived with that oaf Malcolm for more than thirty years? The party on Friday night was put together by Andrew as a bit of a surprise. We took the decision to use it to test the switch on a small group of people, just to see if it would work. To see if anyone would notice if Oscar were to resume his identity again. If it worked, Oscar was going to give up public life and live on his book and TV royalties.'

'You mean Malcolm's book and TV royalties,' Sandy corrected her with a scowl.

'Well, yes. That way we could minimise the chance of anyone ever finding out the truth. God, we'd considered everything: staging a car accident so he could claim amnesia, inventing some sort of dementia-style illness. The details didn't matter — all we knew was that we wanted to be together again. We hadn't planned to kill him that night, but when he came down with that virus it just seemed to make so much sense. It made our job so much easier. When the switch worked and no-one realised Oscar was a different person, we made the decision. It was still a big risk. There was never meant to be a body or any clue anyone had been killed. Not until bloody Dolores Mickelwhite went nosing about at the moment Oscar killed Malcolm. It was just meant to be a simple switching of identities. Switching them back to how they were meant to be. If Malcolm officially never even existed, how could he have been murdered?'

The man in question took up the reins. 'After I'd killed Malcolm, I hid in the spare bedroom nearest the stairs. When Dolores came upstairs and tried the handle, I panicked. Oddly, he seemed to slip away just at that moment. As if he heard her and thought his saviour had turned up. He stopped struggling and that's when I knew he was dead. When Dolores ran downstairs I slipped out of the room and hid in the spare bedroom. Before I went, I locked the door and slid the key back under using a photocopy of some sort of contract that was on the bedside table. I saw it in a murder mystery novel once. I thought it was brilliant. Bloody problem is, so did you.'

'A clever ruse, but not clever enough,' Hardwick said.

'When Eliza suggested that everyone went into the drawing room so she could be alone, the vicar stayed upstairs. Not a bad move, actually, as it meant there was a solid witness there the whole time. All Eliza had to do was make sure the vicar didn't have a view of the bedroom door and that the others stayed out of the way while I slipped downstairs and out into the back garden. Throughout the whole night we made sure Eliza was downstairs in the middle of the party as much as possible, just in case something went wrong. Which it did.'

'Even so, we thought we were watertight. Everyone had an alibi!' Eliza cried.

'The only person who didn't have an alibi for that night, was a man who didn't even exist,' Hardwick said.

'But I escorted him back upstairs!' Harry Greenlaw

said. 'Do you mean to say I was escorting a murderer?'

'It would seem so,' Hardwick replied. 'And did you see him go into his bedroom, Mr Greenlaw?'

'Well, no. He said he needed to use the bathroom first, so I left him to it.'

'Did it not cross your mind that Oscar and Eliza Whitehouse have an en-suite bathroom, and that he wouldn't logically be using the one on the landing?'

Harry Greenlaw thought for a moment. 'I must admit that it didn't.'

The loud sobbing of Eliza Whitehouse permeated the stunned silence.

'I never stopped loving Oscar. The real Oscar, I mean. Malcolm was a lying, misogynistic, philandering pig. Sure, it was rough and exciting in the early days, but then reality set in. I couldn't leave him. How could I? He was the only other person who knew the truth. I couldn't risk my whole world crashing down around me. It was just easier this way. Easier to stick with it and ride it out. I mean, it had its upsides. The money was good for a start,' she said, even emitting a slight laugh.

'But he wasn't the only other person who knew the truth, was he?' Hardwick said, as numerous pairs of eyes began to dart around the room. 'Because after you left the French Foreign Legion,' Hardwick addressed the killer, 'you lived for a while in Cyprus. Didn't you?'

Oscar's eyes flickered momentarily. 'Yes. How did you know that?'

'Oh, just a little bit of backward deduction, Mr Whitehouse. Let me see... do we know anyone else with links to Cyprus? How about you, Mr Karagounis?' Christos Karagounis's eyes met Hardwick's. 'When I first spoke to you, I noticed something a little odd about your accent and turns of phrase. A certain je ne sais quoi, if you'll indulge in my humour. I'm a well-travelled man, Mr Karagounis, and one who can spot a French lilt in a Cypriot accent a mile off. But why would a native Cypriot have a French lilt to his accent? Perhaps you can explain, Mr Whitehouse.'

Oscar sighed and bowed his head once more, resigned to his fate. 'When I left the Legion, I got involved with a French woman. We ended up moving to Cyprus.'

'But that's not all, is it? When you say you "got involved" with a French woman, what you mean is you had a child together.'

'Yes. He was five when we left France for Cyprus. His mother and I split up a few months later and she re-married a Cypriot man. Even though we kept in touch, my son took his surname. When he was eighteen, he changed his forename from Christophe to Christos. Christos is my son.'

Christos Karagounis bowed his head.

'And it was your son, the humble Cypriot gardener, who you sent to work at Westerlea House, in order to feed you information, wasn't it?'

'Yes. He told me about Malcolm and Eliza's relationship and I slowly came to realise that I could put a stop to things. I could finally get the ultimate revenge and win back the woman I loved. So I came back to England. I laid low and eventually made contact with Eliza. The spark was still there and we realised we were both still in love with each other after all those years.'

'So you hatched your plan to kill your brother and reclaim your original identity. And when it all went wrong, the whole plot started to run away with you, didn't it? Malcolm went to see the vicar a few years ago and told him about what happened in the seventies. When you noticed the vicar starting to put the clues together, you realised that the vicar, too, had to die. And when Dolores Mickelwhite saw him at the scene of the vicar's murder... well, what's a third murder when you've already committed two?'

'It was meant to be so easy. We were going to kill Malcolm silently and dispose of the body. Then I could become Oscar again. No-one would ever have known a murder had even been committed! It would have been the perfect murder.'

'Except when you entered your brother's bedroom and began to kill him, you weren't counting on Dolores Mickelwhite walking past the door at that exact moment.'

'Bloody meddling woman! If she had been downstairs like she was supposed to be, Malcolm would be buried under eight feet of topsoil in the rockery by now.'

'And you would be Oscar Whitehouse once again. Except things started to spiral out of control, didn't they? Because your brother's conscience got the better of him and he explained his story to the vicar in confession. The vicar knew Oscar Whitehouse was actually Malcolm Whitehouse, and that's why you killed him.'

Oscar looked at the floor and nodded.

'And when Dolores Mickelwhite got in your way, yet again, by declaring that she had seen Oscar Whitehouse's double at the vicarage on the night the reverend died, you knew that she had to be next.'

Oscar nodded solemnly. As the room began to relax and come to terms with what had happened, he turned with the speed of a gazelle on a lion-covered plain and darted out of the door, knocking both DI Warner and DC Kerrigan to the floor as he did so. Before the two officers could even register what had happened, Hardwick hurdled over the pair and gave chase.

32

The dew had already begun to settle on the grass, making traction difficult, as Hardwick clambered over the uneven terrain on the upper reaches of Tollinghill Common. The pitch-black night meant his only way of following the killer was to listen keenly for his own grunts and heavy footsteps, the moon providing little in the way of natural light. Hardwick felt the lace on his right shoe loosen at the most inopportune time, and he resisted his natural urge to bend down and re-tie it.

As the killer made his way into the woods, Hardwick was thankful for the heavy foliage and dried twigs, which made following the sounds much easier. Exiting the woods on the far side, Hardwick was struck by the glow of the full moon reflecting off the quarry as he stood a few feet from the edge.

'It's over, Oscar,' Hardwick panted. 'Come with me and we can sort everything out.'

'You seem to have underestimated me, Hardwick,' the killer said, trying to catch his breath. 'I'm an escapist. That's what I do. I run away from things.'

'Too much time spent in the French military,' Hardwick quipped, bending over with his hands on his knees. 'You can't run away from this, though. Too much water has passed under the bridge. Do the right thing and hand yourself in.'

'No. You're right,' Oscar said, apparently coming to his senses as he walked towards Hardwick with his arms outstretched, palms up, as if requesting arrest. Hardwick recognised the look in his eyes a moment too late, as Oscar's outstretched arms rammed into his chest, pushing him off balance and onto his back, his body teetering over the edge of the cavernous quarry.

As he struggled to keep his balance and crawl back to safety, Hardwick clambered onto all fours, his eyes fixated on the enormous chalky drop below him. As he managed to avert his gaze from his imminent certain death, Hardwick felt a shadow fall across him as the light of the moon was blocked by the looming figure of Oscar Whitehouse, who stood at his feet.

'I'm trained to kill a man, you know, Hardwick. I

killed in the Legion and I killed in Tollinghill. A nice fitting end to the story, don't you think?'

Hardwick said not a word, instead grunting with angst against his impending death, as Oscar Whitehouse bent down and grabbed hold of his foot. As Oscar widened his legs, Hardwick's breath stopped sharply and both men sensed the quarry edge give way beneath them.

Oscar's grip on Hardwick's ankle tightened as his balance disappeared over the edge of the quarry. Mere nanoseconds later, Hardwick felt time slow as the weight of Oscar Whitehouse's falling body tugged on his ankle. Sensing this was the end, a thousand thoughts flashed through Hardwick's mind as he prepared to meet death.

Just as the jolt of the falling weight of Oscar White-house took hold, Hardwick felt five large digits clasp around his own left hand, the equilibrium restored as time sped up and Hardwick sensed Oscar's grip on his ankle transferring to his right shoe, which promptly slipped off, taking Oscar Whitehouse with it, as both Oscar and the patent-leather Oxford plummeted to the bottom of Tollinghill Quarry.

33

'I think you'll find you owe me one, Hardwick,' DI Warner said as the men both clambered to their feet.

'In addition to solving three murders, Detective Inspector?' Hardwick asked, removing his sock, which was now wet from the dew-soaked grass.

'Yes, well I'm sure we would have got there eventually.'

'Eventually,' Hardwick accentuated. 'Now, if you don't mind, I'm going to have to walk round to the bottom of the quarry.'

'There's no point, Hardwick. It's a two-hundred-foot drop. There's no way he will have survived that.'

'Oh, I'm not worried about him. I want to retrieve my shoe.'

GET MORE OF MY BOOKS FREE!

Thank you for reading *The Westerlea House Mystery*. I hope it was as much fun for you as it was for me writing it.

To say thank you, I'd like to invite you to my exclusive *VIP Club*, and give you some of my books and short stories for FREE. All members of my VIP Club have access to FREE, exclusive books and short stories which aren't available anywhere else.

You'll also get access to all of my new releases at a bargain-basement price before they're available anywhere else. Joining is absolutely FREE and you can leave at any time, no questions asked. To join the club,

head to adamcroft.net/vip-club **and two free books will be sent to you straight away!**

If you enjoyed the book, please do leave a review on the site you bought it from. Reviews mean an awful lot to writers and they help us to find new readers more than almost anything else. It would be very much appreciated.

I love hearing from my readers, too, so please do feel free to get in touch with me. You can contact me via my website, on Twitter @adamcroft and you can 'like' my Facebook page at facebook.com/adamcroftbooks.

For more information, visit my website: adamcroft.net

DEATH UNDER THE SUN

Kempston Hardwick returns in

DEATH UNDER THE SUN

OUT NOW

After solving two particularly tricky murder cases, Kempston Hardwick needs a holiday. At least that's what his friend, Ellis Flint, in his infinite wisdom, believes.

When the pair arrive on the twenty-four-hour Greek party island of Friktos, Hardwick is in his idea of hell. Eventually, he decides to make the most of his holiday and to try to relax.

That is until one of their fellow holidaymakers is found dead in their apartment...

Turn the page to read the first chapter...

It had never occurred to Ellis Flint to put the lid back on the bottle before shaking it, and he cursed his momentary lapse of concentration as he scraped tomato ketchup from the Artex ceiling with a palette knife. Mrs Flint would never have made a mistake like this. Though Mrs Flint was, of course, hopelessly at work.

The ringing of the doorbell jolted Ellis, causing the palette knife to jab into the ceiling and a lump of ketchuppy plaster to plop gracefully into one of the mugs of freshly-brewed coffee that adorned the kitchen table.

Alighting the wooden chair, Ellis made his way carefully across the laminate flooring and towards the front door, careful to avoid getting ketchup on his socks.

Kempston Hardwick was, of course, expectedly early. And Ellis Flint was expectedly late.

Hardwick smiled as he greeted Ellis, who noted the distinct lack of ketchup stains on Hardwick's immaculate clothing.

'I've made you a coffee,' Ellis said, gesturing for his friend to sit at the table as he spooned the customary six sugars into his own mug.

'Of sorts, yes,' Hardwick said, his nostrils flaring as the bitter steam assaulted his olfactory system.

'I know you've always been telling me I should get some decent coffee in, like the stuff you make at home, so I did. Trying this Nescafé stuff now.'

'Yes, well I was thinking perhaps something a little less... granulated.'

'Come off it!' Ellis said, stirring his own coffee as he plonked himself down on the wooden chair. 'You've seen the adverts. It's the same coffee, just in granules.'

'I haven't, actually,' said Hardwick, who didn't even own a television. 'And that wouldn't really go any way to explaining why it's half the price and a tenth of the taste, would it?'

'Do you need to be so snobbish about everything?' Ellis asked, his head bowed slightly at what he saw as a personal affront.

'There's a big difference between being snobbish

and having standards, Ellis. I am not a snob; I just have higher standards than most.'

'If you ask me, it's all down to stress.'

'Stress?' Hardwick asked, one eyebrow raised.

'Yeah, it's in this book I've been reading,' Ellis replied as he leaned over to grab an almost pristine paperback from the kitchen dresser and plonked it on the table in front of Hardwick. 'It says that stress is the silent killer. Usually, other people are the first ones to notice that the stressed person is behaving a little oddly.'

'I see. And you think I've been "behaving a little oddly", do you?'

'Well, no. Sort of. Actually, I don't know what would be considered odd for you, Kempston, but de-stressing never hurt anyone, did it?' The resultant silence would've been obvious enough to anyone else to have signalled Hardwick's disagreement, but Ellis Flint was not just anyone else. So he continued. 'I've been thinking, actually.'

Hardwick made an uncomfortable grunting noise, seemingly at the thought of another worrying brainwave from Ellis Flint. 'Go on...' he said as he eyed the suspicious reddish-white blob floating in his coffee mug.

'Well, like I said, you've had a tough time of it lately, haven't you?'

'No I haven't.'

'Personally, I'd call two murder investigations pretty damned tough,' Ellis insisted, referring to the previous cases on which they'd worked over the past couple of years. The first, the murder of former light-entertainer Charlie Sparks, had given them the cause to meet and become friends. The second, a case involving the murders of three residents in the sleepy market town of Tollinghill, had been particularly taxing.

'Personally, I'd call it my duty to have investigated them,' Hardwick replied. 'Besides which, I fail to see what you're getting at.'

'Well, I just thought you might need a holiday. That's all.'

'A holiday?'

'Yes, Kempston, a holiday. You know, going away somewhere and enjoying yourself. Not moping about Tollinghill waiting for people to die.'

'I do not mope, Ellis,' Hardwick replied. 'Nor do I wait for people to die. If people have the unfortunate habit of dying within my general proximity, I'm rather at a loss to do anything about it.'

Ellis Flint took a sip of his coffee, himself rather at a loss to do anything, having been once again bamboozled by Hardwick's characteristic way with words.

'Anyway, I think a holiday would be a good idea,' he finally said.

'And I don't.'

'But why not? The prices are very good this time of year, for starters. John Tyler's in Shafford have some great deals on at the moment. I saw one deal to Egypt, a fortnight in an all-inclusive resort complex, for just—'

Hardwick's coffee mug hit the coaster a little harder than it usually would have done. 'Ellis, I do not want to go on holiday.'

'At least hear me out, Kempston. I mean, look outside. The weather's grotty in Tollinghill at the moment. Can't you just imagine yourself lying on a beach somewhere? Or sitting on a sun-kissed verandah reading a good book, drinking a nice cold lager?'

Hardwick raised one eyebrow.

'Or a Campari and orange,' Ellis added.

'Yes, I can, and I'm sure it would all be very nice but it really is unnecessary. I don't need a holiday.'

Ellis Flint sighed and stood up to fetch the sugar jar. This was going to be an eight-spoon affair.

'Kempston, you're not exactly short of money are you?'

'I am a man of independent means if that's what you're insinuating, Ellis.'

'Right, well why not splash some of that cash on a nice holiday? Come on! Palm trees and warm breezes, foreign culture and architecture. What more could you want?'

Hardwick thought for a few moments. 'Well, I have always wanted to visit the Catacombs of Kom el Shoqafa in northern Egypt.'

'That's the spirit! So is that a yes?' Ellis said.

'I suppose so, yes. I can go down to John Tyler's this afternoon and see what they've got. Listen. Thank you, Ellis. You're a good man,' Hardwick said, before taking another mouthful of his coffee.

'I can go one better,' Ellis said, whipping a pair of tickets from his trouser pocket with a flourish. 'I bought us two tickets yesterday afternoon!'

The realisation struck Hardwick's considerable brain at the same time as the piece of tomato-stained Artex hit the back of his throat. After much coughing and spluttering, he had regained his composure enough to exclaim just two words.

'*Two? Us?*'

Want to read on?

Visit   adamcroft.net/book/death-under-the-sun/ to grab your copy.

ACKNOWLEDGMENTS

The research that went into this book was far greater than all of my other books put together. However, I cannot take the credit for that. I am eternally indebted to a number of people who gave up their free time to help make *The Westerlea House Mystery* as good as it could possibly be: to Paul Naish, Duty Port Operations Manager at Portsmouth International Port, for his time and priceless historical information on the routes and fleet at Portsmouth Ferry Port in the 1970s (yes, that's why I had to put the acknowledgements at the back of this particular book); to the Reverend Nigel Washington from Westoning Church in Bedfordshire, for his charming nature, fascinating insight into the Church of England and its form and practices, and for putting up with my daft — and probably highly ignorant — questions. I sincerely hope Hardwick's militant (and often insulting) atheism didn't offend.

I must also thank my wife and mother, who are always the very first two people to read my books and offer unabashed constructive criticism. As authors, we are always told never to ask family and friends to offer advice on your books, as they will be naturally too diplomatic. I am fortunate in that both my wife and mother are unwavering in their brutal honesty and will be the first people to gleefully pick my plot to pieces. The subsequent patching and reinforcements put in place will always make for a far better book, and I am hugely grateful to them for their continuing help, time and brutality.

The cover design for the book came from the genius that is David Lovesy, and images of my ugly mug were made almost bearable by the expertise of Gordon Tant Photography and heavy doses of Adobe Photoshop. Thanks also go to Isabel Kelly for all her help with press and promotion. For tidying, polishing and improving the book to be the best it possibly could be, my final and biggest thanks must go to my editor, Libby Calaby, for her eagle eye and unwavering attention to detail.